La   HP
D
                                    ncashire
                                    unty Council

MAMMALS

MAMMALS

Pierre Mérot

Translated from the French
by Frank Wynne

CANONGATE
Edinburgh · New York · Melbourne

First published in English in Great Britain in 2006 by
Canongate Books Ltd, 14 High Street,
Edinburgh EH1 1TE

Published simultaneously in 2006 in Canada by House of Anansi Press,
in Australia by The Text Publishing Company and USA by Grove/Atlantic

Originally published in France in 2003 under the title *Mammifères* by
Éditions Flammarion

1

British Library Cataloguing-in-Publication Data
A catalogue record for this book is available on
request from the British Library

The publisher gratefully acknowledges subsidy from the Scottish Arts
Council towards the publication of this volume

Scottish
Arts Council

This book is supported by the French Ministry for Foreign Affairs, as part
of the Burgess programme headed for the French Embassy in London by
the Institut Français du Royaume-Uni.

 institut français

1 84195 583 3 (10-Digit ISBN)
978 184195 583 4 (13-Digit ISBN)

Typeset in Sabon
by Palimpsest Book Production Ltd, Polmont, Stirlingshire
Printed and bound in Great Britain by CPD Wales, Ebbw Vale

www.canongate.net

To Mireille

And to Dominique and John,
Éric and Élise,
Michèle, Thomas, Valérie,
to Joanna's Poland,
to the nighthawks,
to the inevitable family.

The work which appears on page 66–67 is by
André du Colombier.

I

Erosive Gastritis

I

Every model family should have a fuck-up: a family without a fuck-up is not truly a family, because it lacks an element that challenges it, thereby reinforcing its legitimacy.

The uncle is forty years old and lives in a studio flat thirty metres square, like a child's bedroom without the parents. The space the uncle occupies is inversely proportional to his age: when he was thirty he lived in an apartment fifty metres square.

The uncle wishes his mother would pursue her obsession with disease and her tedious blather in the realm of the dead. Not that a splinter is quite so easily removed from the soul, but the physical passing of a person certainly has distinct advantages.

The uncle has chalked up a gratifying number of fuck-ups that serve to reassure the family in their own just and noble life choices: unemployment, divorce, absence of descendants, cohabiting with divorcées, abortive attempts to fit into single-parent families etc.

The uncle went to the finest institutions but has failed to bear the expected fruit. Because, let us be honest, a child is a long-term investment. In an earlier age – a blessed time – infant mortality took care of the most glaring errors. The uncle's father, an ardent polemicist, harks back with a certain wistfulness to a happier time when, every year, summer wars played their part in wiping out the surfeit of young males. But improvements in medicine and sanitation, and the scarcity of wars between wealthy countries, mean that nowadays it is once again left to the family – behind closed doors and much more discreetly – to choke off the rotten branches. No matter what people say – let us cherish such expressions – a model family is, above all, an engine of selection and gives each new infant a more or less joyous welcome.

Aside from his social failings, the most incontrovertible proof of which has been his shameful lack of children and happiness, the uncle has also amassed a catalogue of archetypal faults: he smokes about forty cigarettes a day – two and a half an hour, if we assume he gets any sleep. He drinks. He is spineless. He is obsessed with sex.

The uncle admirably embodies the fuck-up essential to a family's equilibrium, in that he has avoided – where has he been? – all reproductive function, and offers his nearest and dearest a troubling yet alluring glimpse of exotic dissipation. He is son and uncle, has nieces and nephews, but he cannot in any sense claim to be a father, though at forty the longing for children is almost as painful to him as the longing for a woman;

and yet, for a man of his age, there is a problem – not a physiological problem, of course, but a symbolic one.

As he writes these lines one February morning, he slurps rapturously on a beer with the age-old, heavenly feeling that, despite everything, he is in the right. It is midday. The sun is shining. The cool beer trickles the length of his heart.

II

Where do I begin? This is how bad books, how failed books, begin. But with age and confidence in your own self-worth comes the ability to wield clichés unscathed.

Because the uncle was once important. That, at least, is the myth that has been insidiously kept alive: a family that aspires to greatness inevitably produces a failure of great calibre. The uncle is probably the family's greatest success, an extremely long-term investment for a minimal risk. How many times has he had to listen to how he might have achieved this or that in the realm of things intellectual? But the uncle has no sense of honour, his morning resolutions trickle away like sand by nightfall. His soul is 'indolent and languid', to quote the admirable Portuguese poet and opium-addict, author of a single collection of poems, who left to pursue his agreeable decline in Macao around 1900 with a Chinese woman and a dose of tuberculosis in tow.

Let us look at a model family made up of five members. We note with some astonishment that of the three sons, only one has actively worked to ensure heirs: what family could pride itself on such optimism, such survival instincts? The creation of two human beings has required the group effort of no fewer than six people, if we include the role played by the generous mother the family resigned itself to having to bring in from outside. But we should probably add to the conditions that made such extraordinary fertility possible the ten thousand scholarly books and thirty years of higher education – most of it male – which this productive hive of activity has accumulated.

Human beings have a tendency to pass judgement – generally negative – on others, and to think in hierarchical terms. Obviously, the objective of those who do so is to dominate or believe they dominate, other people. From this point of view, the uncle's family is a highly efficient factory churning out judgements and pecking orders. Its specialized subject is the intellectual. Other families might specialize in money, power or social status. Sometimes, all of these criteria. The intellectual pinnacle of the uncle's family is the eldest son, in whom all investments were concentrated. From their perch up on their rock, as in a zoo, the family hurls curses and commiserates in defeats: the world is divided into entrance exams, universities, grades, noble and common disciplines, careers etc. Let us take an example: you are a teacher. In order to approach Olympus, from whose summit you are watched politely and ironically, you must first satisfy a number of routine criteria – routine, at least, in the opinion of your judge: this entrance examination, that degree course including Latin and Greek, this prestigious *grande école*, that position in your class. Let us assume you overcome these hurdles: you might still find that people suddenly seem vague or give you a pitying smile if they discover that you did not attend the right college at your prestigious university. Which college? *The* college. But let us suppose that you did go to the right college. You are welcomed into the fold, you enjoy a certain relaxed camaraderie. But a second ordeal awaits you: can't you hear the embarrassment in the voice of the person speaking to you? It is simply that your job and the academic papers you have published are perfectly acceptable, but they're hardly what one expects up here on the summit. A summit as mediocre as the hearts of those who think like this.

From this, we can deduce that the uncle loves losers, the disgraced, the suffering, the orphaned. In fact, he was once married to a woman who had the singular advantage of having no family at all. She came from Poland. She was very beautiful and very damaged. The uncle's family thought very highly of her, and rather charmingly called her 'la Polonaise', since Polish women are obviously interchangeable; it is common knowledge that they come to France with only one thing in mind: finding a husband. As for 'the nurse', who supplanted 'la Polonaise', the uncle loved her family because it was the absolute antithesis of his own: the nurse herself was the most highly educated in her family;

one of the others worked in retail, another was an engineer. These charming folk lived in the provinces, drank a little too much, made commendable mistakes in French, were kind-hearted, and, all in all, comprised a family just as shabby as the uncle's own but differently so. For the first time in his life the uncle had brothers-in-law. Anyone who has never had brothers-in-law – those slightly boorish creatures with whom to drink and swap clever, desperate, vulgar jokes – does not truly understand love or life.

At this uncertain beginning of his odyssey, the uncle might seem bitter, insincere, lacking in depth. This is true . . . But he also thinks of himself as a sort of benign and intractable Fate watching from afar over the destiny of his family, all the more fondly since he was cast from that same preposterous, painful, and terribly human mould.

III

If it is possible to die – physically die – for want of love, then the uncle is dying. It may take time, but he will die. Unless something changes, the disease will kill him. Some people die of being unable to love, others of being unloved. Furthermore, anyone who still believes in love – even some simple, unexceptional love – will be the first to be annihilated.

The uncle truly believes that one day he will fall asleep with a drink in his hand on the terrace of a bar and never wake up. He will probably pass away in his sleep, but the coroner will confirm that the disease had run its course: he will have died from an excessive want of love.

The uncle drinks. It is an undeniable fact that the uncle drinks. He does not drink because he is alone: he has brought his fair share of conquests – some scandalous, others not – to the family dinner table. Whether out of defiance or optimism or like a cat offering its kill to its master hoping for some sign of affection or perhaps simply because he thought he could introduce into this essentially unfeminine family something it had always lacked, he has brought at least one-tenth of his quarry to the family table. The rest are dispersed amidst the lechery and mystery of the night.

So, the uncle does not drink because he is alone, but because he wants to be alone. In this, he is probably not so different from other people. Nowadays, we all believe we will wind up alone.

The uncle drinks four litres of beer in an evening. Sometimes more. Beer has the advantage over spirits because it makes you feel as if you can go on drinking forever. The effects the morning after are the same, but the night before, it feels as if you have drunk endlessly. An alcoholic cannot bear to be interrupted. Anything that interrupts him, namely other people and death, is even more unbearable than his own kind.

Alcohol is a complex thing – although those who devote their lives to it are attempting to reduce life to a simple principle.

The drinker portrays drinking as a priceless treasure. Do not believe him. It is abject suffering.

The drinker describes his drinking as a profession. It is true that alcoholism is hard work in that it takes up most of the day, requires a certain aptitude – albeit purely physical – and a knowledge of the varieties of alcohol and their dosage, and is his principle topic of conversation. What is an alcoholic? There are many possible answers, but let us agree on a simple one: an alcoholic is anyone who one day realizes that alcohol is the most important thing in his life. The quantity of alcohol consumed plays a part, of course, but at the end of the day, regardless of quantity, you are an alcoholic when you tell others that alcohol is your chief problem.

Drinkers are part of a brotherhood. Go to a bar and look. Drinkers seek each other out with their third eye. They are quick to recognize their own kind. They exchange smiles. They understand the fine line between heartbreak and joy.

The drinker is an exhibitionist. Alcohol is like a ruby on his finger. His eyes glitter with suffering like a woman with a wedding ring. There he sits, a sliver of night propping up the bar. He has put his suffering on the bar in front of him. He plays with it, turns it idly between his fingers, holds it up to the light. He wants others to see it. It is an offering. He doesn't know what to do with it, so he flaunts it. He is an accomplished martyr, an actor playing at suffering, and that is how he wants others to see him.

The drinker and his alcohol of choice form a series of binary relationships: craving and fulfillment, happiness and guilt, exhaustion and renewal, worry and relief etc. The first of these seems most important so we shall begin there. It is difficult to uncover the origin of the craving without making it seem like something sacred. To understand the alcoholic, we first have to accept that an alcoholic is a perfect machine that secretes a craving every day in order to satisfy it; as soon as it is satisfied, the alcoholic begins to secrete more craving, and so on.

We might offer the following definition: we are addicted to something or someone from the moment it provides us with a thing and its converse, specifically, absolute pleasure and absolute pain.

From these few lines, it should be obvious that alcohol is inextricably bound up with love and ruin.

As a result, the uncle's opinion of love is broadly pessimistic. He once wrote: *Love lasts for as long as it takes to destroy its object.* He was not yet thirty; the phrase smacks of romanticism. If he considers his life now, he would be more inclined to say: any couple embarking on a relationship is harbouring the stowaway of their inevitable separation; in fact, their relationship is nothing more than the gradual, increasingly conscious construction of their impending breakup.

On the subject of sex – love or affection – the uncle has often thought that mankind's tragedy stems from the fact that sex is not as elemental, as involuntary and predictable, as the respiratory and circulatory systems: it is in fact possible to go for a year or more without sex. On the other hand, from the point of view of the species, sex is an absolute necessity. Nowadays, the uncle would temper his remarks: it is possible to die – physically die – of having no one to hold you.

People come together, break up, get back together, break up again. Life ends much as a party ends: single people clinging to other single people they had barely noticed before. This is hardly a recipe for successful long-term relationships.

The uncle has been known to write short pieces on the subjects of love and alcohol: beginnings of novels, scattered poems. The uncle is weak-willed; the uncle does not see things through. He maintains a modest, bourgeois disgrace. So on these troubling subjects he's written only bits and pieces. He would like to find a place for these fragments in this book, if for no other reason than that they inevitably contain some part of autobiography . . .

We loved each other as well as alcoholics can, namely when we had been drinking and the prospect of momentous drama opened up before us. People naturally hope that love will be dramatic. Alcohol makes this a certainty. We drink, and inevitably there is drama. We know that at the appointed hour the theatre of alcohol will not fail us. And if, as we dimly suspect, there is a relationship between alcohol and our lack of love, then there will be magnificence: two people who drink together and try to love together will produce the most demanding crises, will demand everything, will demand that the other be utterly flawed so that love might grow like a unconditional need . . . I met C. in a bar; we were already drunk, but I was holding up better than she was. During her brief drinking binges – she knocked back her drink like murky lightning – she proved herself to be so cruel that she suffered almost as much as I did, demanding to be fucked, to be slapped, tolerating neither delay nor gentleness . . . At times like this she shouted strange things: 'Smother me with prison kisses! Lash me with the trout of death!' . . . She rejected me with increasing brutality, furious in the night, because I insisted she accept other proofs than these acts . . . The terrible proofs we demand of those we love . . . I was just as brutal in my own way. I have always treated love like a court case. The accused in this funereal marriage will never be able to produce the evidence needed to be finally acquitted. The trial is rigged. All innocence will be rejected. The accused will be forced into the wrong. Thus, step by step, I crafted the betrayal of the women I have loved.

IV

What is a bar? More precisely, what is a local? A local is a place you go because you feel terrible and you know that others there feel worse. This means it is a place where you feel particularly good. It is a hospital filled with happy patients hooked up to drips, a profoundly human shit-hole. Let us consider an example: You have taken two or three days of sick leave this year to nurse excruciating hangovers. You are furious with yourself. You swear you will never do it again. The next night, as you are propping up your favourite bar, once more completely in control of your life, someone tells you that Marcus, a jolly man of about fifty you are rather fond of, a podgy civil servant who wears women's stockings under his trousers, has just received an incredulous letter from his manager because he has taken seventy-three days of sick leave this year. The owner of the bar tells you this in a roar of hopeless, humane laughter. Seventy-three days . . . You whistle appreciatively, it makes you feel small, you realize suddenly just what humanity is. Meanwhile, at the other end of the bar, Marcus sits nursing his fifteenth drink and singing; he winks at you,

swaying his hips almost sensually: 'I'll travel everywhere,
to beaches thronged with millionaires, to the last of the
Mohicans, to seedy strip clubs.' He discovered this splen-
did phrase in the dictionary and, giggling, sings it almost
every night. It was Marcus, a civil servant who works
for social security, who taught you the fundamental
maxim: 'When you go to buy alcohol, always buy as
much as possible, because you always end up drinking
more than you expect.' Marcus looks set to miss day
number seventy-four.

A local is usually frequented by a doyenne. People
kiss her on both cheeks as they arrive and as they leave
– always assuming that 'leaving' means anything here:
you come in with some foolish dream of love, but you
never leave. The doyenne has velvet skin. She was beautiful once. Sometimes she talks to you about her
husband, long dead now. The average age of a doyenne
is eighty. The oldest the uncle has met was ninety. Every
night she would drink five or six pastis between seven
and midnight. A doyenne is the guardian angel of the
bar she frequents, and she plays a precise role: she
exists to remind you that alcohol guarantees a long
and happy life. The owner sometimes gives her drinks
on the house. She is often a former bar owner herself
and has never forgotten this wonderful atmosphere of
hell.

You are on intimate terms with at least ten locals.
All are within walking distance of one another, giving
you a choice of different expeditions depending on how

much suffering you wish to inflict upon yourself. Sometimes you wonder which is more important, the drinking or the suffering? You could argue that alcohol is an aggravating factor, but the decision to suffer, to suffer horribly, is one you have already made. There are three-bar nights and seven-bar nights. There are the dawn bars for when you are truly suffering, in other words when you have decided that love, alcohol and loneliness are one and the same. You walk home, eyes fixed on an imaginary line on the pavement, trying not to stumble. You have written dreadful notes to institutional barmaids – those tall, beautiful girls perched on wooden pedestals. Day breaks, bars close, streets are empty, devastated, theatrical, and it is something worse than death. This is why you drink: to be alone with the hopelessness of love.

A local is the sounding board for your neighbourhood, a neighbourhood you quickly begin to realize has more than its fair share of drinkers. You no longer look at people in the street the same way. That girl in the suit, taking money out of an ATM, is not what she appears. The old man with the plastic bag taking tiny rapacious steps is headed for an endless, lonely party. With a drinker's eye, you are better able to interpret your neighbourhood, especially on Sundays. Sunday afternoons have the air of the aftermath following a natural disaster. Walking alongside the families out for a stroll in these deserted streets, sharing the same pavements but living in another dimension, a different

space–time continuum, in mortal coils unimaginable to
ordinary mortals, in shrouds of suffering, are the ghosts
you know only too well. Some have been home to sleep,
others haven't slept at all, and all of them trudge towards
evening as towards some mythic dawn.

Why have you failed in love? You have probably met
someone you could have made a life with, some girl
or some guy who was a bit crazy. It was a long time
ago. You used to drink back then, too, but it was different. You waited for your love on fiery balconies, on
bloated evenings. They would turn up spectacularly
late. You could not bear to watch them sleep, and since
it was summer and they were twenty, you woke them.
Life was one long endless dawn. She was a tall girl, he
was a heavy-set guy with a violent streak, sometimes
they would disappear for days at a time. Oh, you have
had other loves, loves that lasted longer than this. You
are not interested in working out the hierarchy of those
you have loved. You had some glorious moments
between the ages of twenty and thirty, now you believe
you will have no more.

The bar is peaceful, airy, full of light. It is summer.
The awning looks like a giant motherly parasol. There
is a light wind, a scattering of clouds, a faintly mysterious music. The girls are pretty and distant. There is
nothing better than half-empty bars, nights without
number. The man on your left stands silhouetted against
the huge picture window carrying the full weight of his
misery. He is miserable because he is waiting for a

wonderful girl, a tall, beautiful girl who will come and
lean against the bar like an angel or a gaping wound.
You expect nothing. The glasses in the sink quiver like
trout in an old mountain pool. Salesmen pass dream-
lessly selling shoulders to cry on. The barmaid lights a
cigarette because there is no such thing as love. Even
the most determined women, the ones who thought
they could save you, have given up. You feel something
like happiness.

The bar is dark now. The music is of unattainable
lagoons, of lagoons that cannot save you. Night falls
mechanically, stupidly, invincibly. The chandeliers are
pale and uncertain, like old age and dark alleys. Jean-
Baptiste leans on the bar. His wife has thrown him out
as she does every night. They are both alcoholics. He
has been drinking Suze since morning. He works for
the Parks Department. The bars are like blue remem-
bered hills. The mountains of the defeated, the slopes
of the miserable, the low hills of thirst. What can we
expect? A few glasses, a few smiles, a tanned shoulder,
a dirty white bra strap. The music is magnificent. A
singer with a broken voice. If his voice wasn't broken,
nothing would make sense. Hey, Jean-Baptiste, what's
it been – three litres of beer and all those glasses of
Suze? Go home to your wife, Jean-Baptiste, go home
and sleep. But the bar smells of mint and the mint
smells of rum. Why go to bed? Will heaven smell of
mint? Will there be green there? And will our hearts
crack like tinkling ice? Bars open their arms wide like

unfit mothers. They sing to us of lovelessness. This is all we ever wanted. Oh, Jean-Baptiste, let us go to endless bars that never sit in judgement.

But now you are crying on the bar. Why are you crying, Jean-Baptiste? Because you are going to die? Because all things come to an end? You drink, and alcohol feeds your tears. Your life is a pathetic tragedy. But if you had to live it over, the same tragedies, the same mistakes, the same small dewdrops of joy, you would lick it straight from the lips of some two-bit god. You were born and so you are entitled to the resurrection. Soon you will go home and fall asleep beside your imperfect wife, in the scent of cheap shampoo. You will press your lips to exasperating shoulders and tumble, eyes closed, among your stars, and it will be better than anything you have ever known.

Sleep is too much like death, that's why you drown your sorrows in this trivial, raucous, paralytic night. The cellar where the beer barrels snore should become a mausoleum where all the local alcoholics could be buried. You tell the barman this and he roars with laughter because he had the same idea himself. The barman's father hanged himself when he was a teenager. He was the one who cut him down. He keeps a book of the dead: *Jackal*, a sixty-year-old man who used to come in with his dog every night and who refused to quit drinking even when he became ill; Boris, a forty-year-old Yugoslav who used to do odd jobs around the neighbourhood before he started visibly to lose weight from day to day; old Dédé, who walks the streets, slower and slower, on gangrenous feet.

You must never give up drinking. An empty glass means death. The uncle's mother only drinks water, but even she refills her half-full glass if someone mentions death.

The barman roars his huge laugh. Where would he find room for them all? This dynasty of Pharaonic drinkers and mediocre lives – for when we lack greatness, alcohol lends us its own. The cross-dressing civil servant, the mad failed artist, the prostitute who drank so much she had to be carried home, the befuddled old Hungarian man, the parched bric-a-brac sellers, and every girl who has ever spent a night here propping up the bar.

The barman roars his huge laugh because no matter how numerous we are, it is there that we will come when life's cruel joke is over, when we miss everything we once had, but most of all when we miss the alcohol that climbed the rough and stony pathways, the obliging and glorious byways of this body that has been the death of us.

V

A body is a thing composed entirely of words. As science occasionally reveals, it is a poetic construct. Let us watch a routine endoscopy as it takes place. Note that the oesophageal mucous membrane presents itself as normal throughout its length. The cardia is located thirty-eight centimetres from the dental arch. This callous and costly detail explains your true being. The mucosal lake of the stomach is clear. This is a lake far more precious than Baikal. Lake Baikal is the largest reservoir in the world. The uncle is a vast reservoir of alcohol. On pathetic, human Sundays people come here to fish for joy and discontent. There are snack bars and french fries. People go boating, steering yellow and red pedalos towards the leafy shade and the laughter. These delightful attractions account for the exuberant size of his belly. You might spend some time in the neighbouring cardiotuberosity. Here, the mucus is abundant whether viewed live or in playback. There are lovely campsites near the pylorus. The proximal and post-bulbar regions are breathtaking. There are seven hundred documented waterfalls and as many pine forests for brief lives. Ramblers brave the woody scents, a sensible ordinary hobby. Children laugh. But the tour guides advise against venturing into the antrum, an angry, red-raw volcano, characterized by oedematous prepyloric folds and sporadic erosions. There is another inflamed crater in the bulbus duodeni, showing large congestive folds speckled with erosive lesions. Wise tour guides initially diagnosed erosive prepyloric ulceration pending further tests. These are those tests . . . On this December day, the birthday of the body being probed, we take the stipulated biopsies of the antrum. Histological analysis of the antral mucus is characterized by an oedematous, congestive chorion and an epithelial layer pitted with abrasions. The glands appear normal, with no signs of dedifferentiation, dysplasia or metaplasia. There are no signs of heliobacter pylori. This body, whose worries, whose discontents, whose perfunctory hygiene and deviant practices we do not presume to judge, is clearly suffering from acute erosive gastritis in one of its glorious byways. He will be relieved to find out that we found no evidence of a tumour. This body is much the same as the majority of bodies we examine these days. In anticipation of old age or some hypothetical last judgement, we cannot recommend too strongly that he placidly carry on his life of alcohol, tobacco, coffee and effervescent anxiety.

VI

The uncle consults a psychiatrist. A fine psychiatrist who performs no miracles, does no damage. The man is a hypochondriac. He has given up smoking because he is terrified of cancer. He's in the middle of a divorce. While the uncle talks, this amiable man watches his every move, his gestures. The uncle once asked why he did this. The psychiatrist is a behaviourist: gestures and body language offer precious information about your psychological makeup. For example, if you sit on the edge of your seat, hands tensed, gripping the armrests, this brilliant therapist might deduce that you want to leave.

Behaviourists are not interested in listening to your life story. A history of your fears and your alcoholism is of little interest to them. If you suffer from arachnophobia, they will not look to discover the cause; instead, they will gradually force you to confront a hairy trap door spider. This way, you will no longer be afraid of spiders, you will be afraid of body hair, poppies or Japanese restaurants. Behaviourists unsuccessfully try to hypnotize you. They insist on talking about beaches.

All behaviourists have learned the same incantation at some behaviourist seminar or from a copy of *Psychology for Dummies*. Let us listen to a behaviourist: 'You're walking along a beach . . . You feel sand beneath your feet . . . The sand is warm . . . You walk along the beach, and as you walk along the beach, concentrate on your right hand . . .' While the droning voice recites the contents of a travel brochure, the uncle fondly watches as the psychiatrist dozes off. Still, it has to be said that behavioural psychiatrists have one significant advantage over yoga teachers and psychoanalysts: they prescribe antidepressants, although usually only after some slightly theatrical hesitation.

A psychiatrist's waiting room is a very reassuring place. Just sit there for five minutes and you will feel yourself starting to get better. The woman lying prostrate on the sofa ignores your friendly, cheerful greeting. She has bags under her eyes, her fingernails are bitten to the quick. Compared to her, you feel fine. You could leave right now. The session would not have cost you a penny. But stay a while and listen. Your therapy continues. The psychiatrist's consulting room is next to the waiting room. You hear screaming, a long silence, then sobbing. Some woman is having a breakdown. You can hear her off in the distance. Unfortunately, you cannot quite make out what she is saying. But it hardly matters, you are feeling better already. The psychiatrist's door opens and a curious cortège emerges: a pathetic man of about fifty leads the way; he's followed by a teenage boy wearing headphones; last comes the grief-stricken woman. Family therapy. Your regular visits to the waiting room have made you an expert. With one single glance, you have diagnosed their problem: the father is a nonentity, a puny little runt who probably visits prostitutes' websites; the son probably withdrew into a disturbing silence at the onset of puberty; the mother, teetering on the brink of divorce, is sinking deeper into depression every day. You would like to talk to them, tell them you feel their pain, that you have even worked out the solution: there is a gunsmith nearby who sells top-quality hunting rifles. Instead, you stand there and, smiling, give your psychiatrist a knowing look. Your first words will be: 'They're in a bad way!' The psychiatrist concurs: the son did not take his headphones off during the session, the father did not say a single word, and the mother cried, all for a tidy sum. You, clearly, are in perfect health.

What is a panic attack? A typical panic attack lasts about two hours. You feel as if you are going to die. In themselves, panic attacks are not life-threatening. If, on the other hand, you have two or three panic attacks a week, you begin to contemplate suicide. Panic affects a growing number of people, though most, thankfully, are not attacked by it. Alcohol is an excellent tranquilizer, though later trigger, for panic. It is an aggravating factor in an already panicked subject. There are many reasons to panic: genetics, education, modern life, unsolvable personal conflicts etc. The air you breathe, the sounds you hear, the things you see every day are teeming with anxiety. Your body absorbs this escalating series of alarm signals. These are symptoms of the world. The world you're part of is in a bad way. It is stupid, aggressive and hostile. The French lead the world in the consumption of tranquilizers.

The uncle consulted his first psychiatrist twenty years ago, while he was doing his military service in idyllic tedium in Paris. Things got off to a bad start: the man was his mother's psychiatrist, an overbearing old codger whom she thought of as her father, and who manfully cured her nervous breakdown brought on by her inability to deal with menopause. The uncle's first consultation with this psychoanalytic grandfather was rowdy. The uncle was twenty-two. He was suffering from panic attacks, though he did not know this. He was terrified by these new, ill-defined, but altogether frightening symptoms.

The uncle has problems with authority or at least authority that goes beyond the bounds of the rational. It is probably old-fashioned to believe in the rational these days, but that is how he is. It is true that the uncle is fascinated by power. But it is just that: fascination. For example, he likes, aesthetically likes, Milton's line: *Better to reign in Hell than serve in Heav'n.*

At the age of twenty-two, the uncle was already a whisky drinker. He had also tried hashish on several occasions. His new ersatz grandfather, who was a Jew, lectured him. There was no mention of symptoms, still less of causes. For the former senior consultant of

Charenton Asylum, the causes were patently obvious, and he had no intention of divulging them. It might have been interesting, though, to try to discover why the uncle had taken to drink so young. Similarly, it might have been productive to discuss the events of the delicious Saturday that preceded his very first panic attack: why had his mother's lesbian cousin chosen that very Saturday to kill her long-term lover with a hunting rifle before decorating the walls with her own brains, and in doing so further upsetting the uncle who, an hour earlier, had had all his hopes dashed by the girl of his dreams? But the ersatz grandfather simply bellowed: 'You must never touch a drop of alcohol again!' And then roared: 'Hashish!!!' Then he delivered a lecture on the etymology of the name of this ruinous drug, which essentially consisted of an invective against the 'Secret Order of the Assassins', a society regrettably made up of Arabs.

'Yes, but . . .' said the uncle, 'what about the symptoms? What about the cause?'

'You are not to touch another drop of alcohol! You must immediately cease all consumption of hashish!'

One year later, after a small-scale hell of panic attacks, constant illness, anxiety and turmoil, the foolish quack let slip his magnanimous diagnosis: 'You suffered a slight nervous breakdown.'

The man has probably died since. Best thing he could do.

VII

Seen from the outside, the uncle's love life probably seems vast and luxuriant. In fact, it is a joke. The uncle usually finds himself dealing with two or three women whose stated goal is to make him happy or – even better – to save him. They usually admit defeat after a few weeks. Others are looking for someone to father a child before it is too late. Some are attracted by the very impossibility of love. They quickly find themselves cast as defendants in a Kafkaesque trial: the uncle resents them because he is not in love with them. But the uncle is not a monster. Like a company laying off staff, he always offers them a way out. He uses a heart-warming turn of phrase: 'You deserve to find someone who can really love you', or 'I've got a friend who's a depressive alcoholic, maybe I can introduce you . . .'

At some point – this is only natural – the uncle will receive bitter, contemptuous letters. If he thought they were of public interest, he would index them and publish an anthology. But what criteria to use? The letters range from exasperation to fury, from despondency to belligerence, from mawkish advice to ruthless judgement. It might be more interesting to index the letters according to whether or not they arrive with corroborating evidence, i.e., whether or not they come with extracts from unidentified authors – generally photocopied – in which the cruellest phrases have been lovingly underlined. These extracts are offered as evidence – the weight of an entire culture – in support of the prosecution's case. After all, we all try to elevate less exalted souls to our lofty understanding of humanity and the world. Let us take an example, a forty-something we will call 'the Scorned Woman'. The uncle, probably feeling the worse for wear after a night on the tiles and elegantly dressed in a grubby, tattered dressing gown, receives one of the aforementioned photocopies in the morning post. It is an extract from *La Condition Ouvrière* by Simone Weil, specifically a passage from 'Letter to a student'. This is an unfair fight: no fewer than three women are lined up here to settle scores with the uncle. In passing, note that many women consider this incomparable victim of tuberculosis (who allowed herself to die in a London sanatorium in the middle of a world war, out of solidarity for the human race) to be a staunch moral guide or even a Christ figure with glasses and a vagina. The uncle farts to steel himself, his vision is a little blurred. Maybe he remembers that in the early hours in a bar just as blurred he was chatting with a primary school teacher about the education system and he called her a 'stupid cow'. But probably not. Drinkers seem to spend their evenings in another dimension. They wake next morning, maybe next afternoon, with a monstrously swollen finger and no memory of falling down a flight of steps. Steps are the chief enemy of the alcoholic, particularly those shockingly narrow, dark stairs in bars. The fall took place as though in a dream. The uncle, who is, we should emphasize, only a small-time drinker, remembers waking up to the strange spectacle of nocturnal noodles, clearly abandoned during the cooking process, floating in a saucepan of cold water. Nothing strange so far. But atop the noodles floated a two-hundred-franc note. The uncle has no explanation for this. Details like this make you realize you are in a bad way, a farcically bad way. It seems obvious, therefore, that the uncle does not feel entitled to judge other people.[1] But let us get back to

---

[1] About these much-vaunted steps, the uncle composed the beginnings of a faintly grandiloquent, mercifully unfinished poem:

> God is fifteen steps and broken fingers
> fifteen bars each night
> a wall of panic tumbling into urine
> into tears
> God waits below for alcoholics
> wearing a greasy apron
> climbing to unbolt the dawn with fists flying
>
> Oh, muscles
> Frozen lion cubs
> I come with harp-filled wine!
>
> This is the bar where sorrows rest their elbows
>
> Bulls upon the high stools of solitude

Simone Weil. The uncle reads the passage which has been lovingly underlined. This, then, is what Simone and the Scorned Woman think of the uncle: 'There are people who have lived nothing but sensations and for sensations . . . They are, in truth, life's fools and, as they themselves confusedly sense, they tumble constantly into deep sadness where they find themselves without any other recourse than to deaden their sorrows and wretchedly deceive themselves.' At this point in his reading the uncle is supposed to collapse on the imitation parquet of his studio apartment, victim of an affective infarction. Then comes the second extract, underlined with equal affection by this woman who is no more in control of her life than the uncle is of his: 'The search for sensation implies an egotism that, personally, I find loathsome. Clearly it does not prevent one from loving, but it leads one to think of loved ones merely as occasions of joy or pain, forgetting completely that they exist in themselves. One lives among ghosts. One dreams rather than lives.' And Simone goes on: 'As regards love, I have no advice to give you . . .' Hence the trial. There follow four or five lines from the Scorned Woman, in beautiful handwriting, drawing the uncle's attention to his reprehensible behaviour and maybe to his monstrous personality. The trial concludes with the following impressive sentence: 'I think maybe we shouldn't see each other any more.' The uncle belches in terror. The word 'maybe' clearly demands pause. It doesn't bode well. It is clearly only the start of a series of recriminations which will escalate with her suffering – suffering this beautiful woman could have spared herself if only she had gone for a clean break.

The uncle also meets girls he would like to save. They are usually young and wild, as drunk as he is at six in the morning. Some are prostitutes, but even they talk about love and nostalgically reminisce about their schooldays. The uncle is regularly pestered by one of these. She phones him during school holidays. She has obviously got a sizeable little black book of teachers. She is a specialist: she knows exactly when they will be most vulnerable. The uncle never phones back, although once, one distant and disastrous dawn, they had a fascinating conversation about love and stylistic devices; in particular she amazed him with her knowledge of the zeugma. The uncle is none too fond of prostitution, not from any strict moral code but from lack of funds. There are young middle-class girls he would also like to save, but they are too scared. Let us consider an example. A woman of about thirty has just entered the bar. The uncle makes advances on her, his voice slurred and sociable. She politely moves away. This is obviously a mistake. If she were to get involved with a forty-year-old alcoholic, a psychic and psychological wreck, it would spare her the unpleasant shock of watching her current lover – a boy her own age whom she adores – get flabby; watch him bloat, fart, sweat, belch, lose his hair, spill wine on his tie, start to smell of liver disease, become lecherous and belligerent,

produce sperm the colour of Kronenbourg and intellectually – always assuming he has a brain to begin
with – turn into a cross between computer analyst and
middle-manager, rabid right-wing thug and eco-warrior,
Taliban and chimpanzee. With a forty-year-old, there
are no such surprises: most of the work has been done.
Besides, she would only have to put up with him for
ten short years, because the moment he turns fifty and
reaches the peak of his powers, and finds himself saddled
with a forty-year-old woman suffering from cellulite
and approaching menopause, an erotic marvel dressed
in canvas hiking boots and sanitary napkins, the man
will cast her aside and turn his attentions to the younger
generation. But this young woman is incapable of
making long-term decisions.

This still leaves two or three devoted admirers who
generally confide in the uncle thus: 'I'm living with this
guy, but I'm not sure I love him.'

Let us take the case of Ophelia.

Ophelia was thirty-five. She had just married her
boyfriend of ten years, a happy event which triggered
a sudden, cruel revelation: she didn't love her boyfriend,
she had never loved him, he wasn't *exciting* enough.
They had been trying for a baby methodically now for
ten years, but nothing came of it. She was quite pretty,
although she had terrible dress sense. Her intelligence
and general knowledge were those of a typical secondary school teacher. She loved Louis de Funès films. She
talked about them a lot. But her favourite topic of

conversation was love. She had more or less fallen in love with the uncle, in whom she detected the quintessential virile and *exciting* male. She was seduced by the uncle's gentle disposition: she was rather surprised when he knocked back three beers and two kirs on their first date, but in the end she decided that this simply made the uncle more *exciting*. Because Ophelia was horribly bored. Professionally and emotionally. In fact, she had been planning to quit teaching to fulfill her childhood dream of working at the cosmetics counter on the ground floor of the *Galeries Lafayette*. It is worth noting that many teachers consider quitting after fifteen years. The uncle, on the other hand, has only been teaching a short while and is overjoyed with this new and charming profession. But let's get back to the nymphomaniac. Falling in love with another teacher must have seemed like the perfect solution. The uncle had turned up at precisely the right moment. Suddenly, Ophelia's dreary school was turned into an oriental harem prowled by a dark, brooding, alcoholic sultan. She began to dream up work-related fantasies. She would ask the uncle if she could sit in on his classes. 'I'll be quiet as a mouse,' she'd say. And she proved to be very quiet and terribly refined. She would creep up to him and yell: 'You know I always have to bring a spare pair of knickers with me, because every time I see you . . .' Or she would lie on the staff room sofa and say: 'I don't suppose you fancy fucking me right here, right now?' The uncle felt a little awkward. She only propositioned him verbally, however. Ever since the uncle lovingly confessed that he wasn't *quite* in love with her, she refused to sleep with him. But once she stayed the night at his house, allowed him to see her naked, only to brutally reject him when he slipped a dexterous finger into something moist. The uncle wisely declined to ravish Ophelia. As the weeks went by, he avoided her more and more. She left notes in his pigeonhole, notes that were both amorous and vacuous. In one final burst, she proposed 'fellatio, under the desk, room 209'. It was to be his birthday present, the note specified. After that, they avoided each other completely. If he had felt anything at all for Ophelia, the uncle would now be a family man, spending his time eating soup, watching Louis de Funès films, and rampantly fucking some neurotic in empty classrooms.

Nowadays, life has convinced us we can split up with someone and find love in abundance. This of course is a lie. Love is the exception. Lovelessness is the rule. To accept this rule is to take the first step towards happiness.

Though we are all in the same boat, anyone who talks about it is immediately accused of being smug. Look around you: emotional suffering is on the increase, and dating agencies are making a killing. Dating agencies keep alive the illusion of 'meeting someone' in the hearts of those who have no time to meet anyone. In any case, any man who has mastered the contemptible art of the pickup line will tell you that 'meeting people' is not the problem: he meets lots of women and the more women he meets, the more disappointing he finds them. Hearts circulate from bed to bed like worthless banknotes. So to those among you quietly plotting the breakup you are convinced will set you free, those of you who think love – true love – is all around, like so many models in a catalogue whose pages only your partner keeps you from turning, think again: all around you the cutthroat market of lovelessness holds sway.

Without presuming to pronounce on the destiny and disappointments of everyone, there are those who quickly realize that love is the key, those who gradually come to accept that fact, and those who will probably never recognize it. Lives are made and unmade based on this central theme. The uncle falls into the second category. Broadly speaking, if he were thirsty, he would claw the earth with his bare hands to find a spring before it was too late. Unfortunately, the spring always turns out to be within himself and is therefore beyond his reach.

We never stop loving those we once loved. But as we move from person to person, from piece to piece, we try to convince ourselves that we are slowly putting together a jigsaw that will some day show us the true face of love. And then our search will be over. But the only complete picture we have is the most recent, and that image hasn't completely erased the ones that came before. No face is forgotten, none charms us completely. Our lives, therefore, are not a succession of failures, but an unsteady edifice devoted utterly to love.

Wars are waged, loneliness pitted against loneliness. The wounded fight each other with love as the prize. What we resent about others is not the fact that they suffer as we do, but that they have found the same cure. Love is believing that the other person has found a different cure, something that might truly heal us. But most of the time, we clash with people who are just like us, whose pain is just like ours; this is why they are invincible.

VIII

Nobody can live permanently as part of a couple. Those who do so are not wonderful romantics but profoundly depressed individuals. This is an incontrovertible fact, one which should guide our behaviour, whether positively or negatively.

In ten years, the uncle has twice attempted emotional suicide. What is an emotional suicide attempt? To begin with, it typically lasts an exceedingly long time. Thinking back over his life, over the last ten years, the uncle finds himself in possession of a peculiar marriage to a fascinating Polish woman that lasted about four years – something of a record for him. His second attempt – a divorcée gifted with three children and a charming patio – lasted almost as long, but was spiced up by several breakups.

It is therefore obvious that a perfect emotional suicide would last the whole lives of two originally normal individuals. The uncle cannot help but include one or two of the revealing and delightfully – or perceptively? – naive comments made by some of those responsible for these great suicides. Comments which are as revealing about the speakers as they are about the willing victims they ambushed all those years ago and have long since forgotten, since they now behave as though they are living with a ghost or some bulky, clapped-out domestic appliance. The uncle overheard the first of these remarks at the family dinner table; it is the handiwork of his mother. In front of her children and her deaf husband, she gaily announced: 'If I hadn't met your father, I'd have bought a poodle.' The second is more famous – there are echoes of it in Freud – and was recounted to the uncle by his best friend, whose grandmother, talking about her marriage to her husband, used to say: 'When one of us dies, I'll buy a telly.' It is impossible to miss what these two statements have in common: in both cases, a lifetime companion is considered to be a form of entertainment, something easy to control and completely interchangeable, since the life expectancy of a poodle and a television are about the same.

Emotional suicide merely involves spending a long time with someone who affords us little happiness. Someone with whom, at best, you might discuss what to have for supper and affect some childlike joy in doing so. Someone who will listen to you talk about your passions or more prosaically about how your day went, with a forced smile, while secretly deliberating the same question you are asking yourself: when am I going to leave? At best, you will have spent a few short weeks, a few short months in love. Perhaps you will still occasionally use this person as a sex object, maybe

even inadvertently derive some pleasure from him or
her. And both of you will claim that the reason for
your unhappiness is that your partner does not really
love you.

IX

She went back to Poland. They haven't seen each other for years. She phones from time to time. Her voice still has that slightly sad, amused tone, the same insistent voice of the exile, its flags furled somewhere over there in that far-off night. She calls up her ex-husband. Calls up a failure only he can understand. Calls France, Paris, Barbès. Calls up the years spent in dirty, crowded streets fragrant with spices. And he sees her auburn silhouette again, and failure whistles through his blood, sees the black Warsaw crows like fatal blood clots, People's Square, the trams, the cold, the measureless snow. It is enough to make you cry, because when love goes so badly wrong the wound is an ever-open flower.

The uncle is not a traveller. One or two unadventurous trips through wealthy, unscathed Europe. And then Poland. It was two years after the fall of the Berlin Wall. The uncle's first winter holiday is almost a fairy tale. Forgive him his lies and his flights of hyperbole.

It took twenty-four hours for the train to reach Warsaw before it disappeared into darkest Russia. The magic began at the Gare du Nord, where a three-hour delay plunged you immediately into another world: imperturbable, incompetent and elegant. The train stood off to one side, as though on a shameful line. As soon as you saw it, you knew this was your train, the train headed for Warsaw and on towards the Urals and massed horizons. During the Christmas holidays, exiles returned to snowbound families. You wondered how all this luggage would fit into the compartments, all the luxury items born of Prisunic, of the weeping suburbs. 'We'll manage, we'll manage,' your wife told you. She was a little nervous. She was carrying the large sack of bargain-basement gifts, the treasures of the Occident. This despite the fact that her family was minuscule. People die a lot in Poland. More so than in France. Her parents were dead. All that was left was a sister, a brother-in-law and their children. You had bought almost-posh wine. Far away over there in the night, you would lovingly dazzle high society. You walked in silence past the Russian carriages. The Russian carriages were grey, deafening hulks. Luckily, you didn't have to travel in one. Here you stood in front of a brand-new Polish carriage. The wife was wary. She suspected some lavish oversight. She had come to know deprivation ten years before, when it was five degrees Celsius in the kitchen, the warmest room in her tiny state apartment. Her mother was still alive back then and would cross the pitch-black Warsaw winter on foot. The wife was right. There was no heating in the pristine coach. The uncle was even more delighted. His heart blazed, his mind drew him like a magnet towards this country as to a tall, flickering candle.

And so they boarded the icy carriage, fresh from the factories of 'To Your Good Health!'. Passengers armed with screwdrivers were busying themselves around the main radiator. The conductor was already drunk. He was selling Russian watches, booze, half-price tickets, anything and everything. 'Go see the train driver!' The driver stank of vodka. 'Nobody's perfect . . .' he said sleepily. Then there was the Russian carriage with the jammed axle. The heating problems were trivial. An engineer's error. It was five o'clock. There would be a two-hour delay before departure. The driver passed his bottle round and picked up a guitar. And so grim ballads about the battle of Stalingrad and Comrade van Paulus were sung, followed by 'In a small Gdansk Café': *In a small Gdansk café /Ah, my old friend! / the milisk came* . . . The other platforms spluttered, the trains for Sarcelles, for Belgium leaving on time, not heading into the cold. At about seven o'clock, the rail authorities finally put an end to this disgraceful state of affairs. The driver was hoisted into the engine car. The great steel hulk, all the drunken souls, everything lurched off together into the hours and hours before them, drawn towards this country of leather and corruption.

In the freezing carriages, people got acquainted. There was a hard-working couple who seemed old. They were exiles, people of few words. They hated the Poles who stayed at home, mistrusted the French, and were not particularly fond of each other. This was hardly surprising: these were lost generations. The uncle's wife, this sad, beautiful pure-blood, was also quiet. But after a while everyone took out a bottle of something. The exiles perked up. The exiles were syntactically impoverished. Five hundred words brutally strung together with infinitives, the product of twenty years of living in metropolitan France. But it was enough. There are too many words in the West, far too many. Five hundred is more than enough. For the rest, body language, tears, frowns and awkward smiles will suffice.

The train made unscheduled stops in the deserted countryside. People started trafficking. After a three-hour delay in the beetroot fields straddling France and Belgium, the rustic Poles climbed aboard the luxury carriage with blankets and Hungarian champagne on tap. All night the guitar thundered somewhere at the front of the carriage. You enter a country through its music, it is like tasting its blood.

The uncle was a little drunk. The hard-working couple produced an endless stream of bottles. Inroads were made into the stock of French bottles.

Then the train arrived in surly Germany. There were policemen with long hair. Long-haired policemen are the most dangerous. They still post rewards at the border for their great men. Being an informant, playing Judas, still works pretty well here. 'Me terrorist!' roared Wyborowa, an old Polish man who'd had carnal knowledge of the Nazis while being suckled with anti-Semitism at his pretty mother's breast. Absent-mindedly, the Sans-Souci beat him senseless. As children of the Enlightenment, children of the French Republic, a ghostly generation born into the lap of luxury, we obviously handle the Germans more tactfully: 'Greetings, comrades of the EEC, companions in the single market, glorious joint managers in the European enterprise!' yelled the uncle, brandishing his American Express card. 'He's only an old Polack, an old Polack . . .' The vague brawls, the bloodless fighting petered out under an ashen sky. We set off again.

In East Germany, homeland of Bach-the-collectivist, the train was attacked by no one knows who, but they certainly weren't democrats. The Poles, armed with sabres, acquitted themselves magnificently.

'Snow, snow!' cried the uncle suddenly.

Snow with white vodka claws. A line of silver birches stretching out forever like upright tears. Huge pipelines running alongside the tracks carrying the hot water for the five-year plan.

One after another, we lost the exiles to forest train stations. Sobbing, they headed off in tiny cars with the remnants of their families, towards their farms.

We finally arrived in the immensity of Warsaw Central Station to a power failure and flickering candles. It was truly magical. The wife walked on ahead, nervous and a little tipsy, her dread of the East flooding back. A vast, ghostly, incurable dread. 'Keep an eye on your zlotys,' she shouted across the dark concourse, looking sinister and Slavic. But the uncle was enchanted, his every sense alert despite twenty hours of neat vodka. In the distance, a giant and a dark-haired woman were waving pleasantly. They both wore imitation bearskin hats. The French husband, they decided, was very nice. *Very nice.* The uncle and the brother-in-law communicated in a strange language made up of Latin, faulty English and goodwill. Somehow everyone piled into the Fiat 500 in a gale of winter laughter, then foot to the floor through the vast, snowbound boulevards of Warsaw the gargantuan. It was –20° and everyone was glowing with health. It was Christmas Eve, the night that Christ was born among the barrels of herring and vodka.

Soon the company arrived in the overheated three-room apartment swathed in the aroma of Christmas, of good simple food. The television was full of song and Christmas trees. Over there, Christmas is a serious business.

Vodka, torrential and various, is sold in unresealable bottles, which means you have to down it all. After a while, the philosophical problem of the self becomes a simple one: the self is that through which, fluvial and transcendent, the endless liquid flows. The uncle proved himself more Polish than the Poles at this game. Could this be the perfect country, a country of inveterate alcoholics and superior incompetence?

The next day, great crows appeared on the snow-covered wastes ringed with Soviet architecture. They reminded the uncle of trips to grain silos as a child. In fact, everything here reminded him of his childhood, of France in the sixties with its basic shops and primitive cars. Unless things changed, the exhilarating future of these people was clear: little by little they would clutter up their country with more and more pointless bits and pieces, as little by little the uncle's ancestors had done with the help of the United Stores.

They visited friends. The husband was an engineer. He earned a good salary, thirty million zlotys. He barely slept. He worked a fifteen-hour day. He was rebuilding Poland. He was equipped with a professionally unemployed prolific breeder. They had a young daughter. She was missing a lung. She coughed in the distance. The breeder gazed approvingly at the uncle. She assumed he was a professional consumer, a fascinating vocation she was keen to master. She collected French magazines. She'd decorated the apartment in the very latest Western style: lots of white, lots of empty space. They were trying for a second child. One with two lungs. All over the country, embryos stirred. Everywhere there were mail-order catalogues, mortgages and plans for expansion. The future, which is always better while still uncertain, is unaware of the price to be paid in emotional and commercial terms, debts that will have to be repaid in the hard currency of neurosis.

The uncle felt charged with a counter-revolutionary mission. He sang the praises of the hardship, the rickety trams, the basic shops, the gloomy markets and the Czech beer. Though in France he was unemployed, here he was a millionaire and insisted on paying for everyone. His enthusiasm got on their nerves. 'Friends, what are a man's needs?' he retorted. 'The bare minimum. Starting with a pig, the acknowledged animal of all sensible peoples . . .' He continued his eulogy to the pig in a nearby delicatessen with a hundred grams of red vodka – the one that makes you horny. The uncle climbed onto a barrel and harangued them: 'Comrades, look at us, what have we achieved during the fifty years you were trapped in the bear's maw? Two magnificent inventions: the remote control and the remote control cover!' It was a bad example since over there – as in Barbès – there was a feverish flowering, a second Prague Spring, with satellite dishes blossoming on every balcony, every rooftop. Televisions blared day and night, a great glow in the west. It was Babel, mostly in German. Now reunified, Poland's neighbour, its old acquaintance, was back and wielding impressive artillery, firing a constant salvo of advertisements, its three battalions blasting into every zloty-pinching home. In this game for consenting adults, France remained considerately pathetic, deploying only TV5, a small army, a single battalion with little firepower in the form of advertising. This is how markets are lost.

In the evenings, they were magnificently alcoholic but bursting with health. Cold is the invention of serious drinkers. It instantly dispels a hangover. So it was in the evenings that the serious business began, a great dialogue with winter, alcohol and politics.

The brother-in-law was twenty-seven and already a spokesperson for the Ministry of Defence. A young, liberal, devoutly Christian generation was starting to take the place of their dishonourable elders. He'd written a book under a pseudonym. He hunted down people with suspicious pasts. The electrician president stood accused of having been some sort of Soviet spy. The uncle made naive, sacrilegious pronouncements on the great communist idea, but an entente of cheerful mumbo-jumbo reigned between the two brothers-in-law. Linguistic ignorance is the mother of simple, affectionate opinions. No one gets hurt. It is when people understand each other that quarrels and wars erupt. Journalists and friends of all sorts traipsed through the sparkling three-room apartment, the warm and festive womb. Within a week, the uncle felt as if he had met every Pole in Poland. He was introduced as the 'Francuz', the Frenchman. That was enough. The uncle, an unemployed millionaire, was seriously considering settling down in this land of the consonant, in this great white land where angels burn and booze. After the evening collation, they took snowy paths to heavy wood apartments bearing poppy-seed cakes, rich salads and the Holy Sacrament – the plastic bag from which, huddled together, singing in the darkness, came the bottles of ice-cold vodka that would soon trickle down throats like a kiss from an incestuous bear, in a delirium of joy, in a philanthropic feast where death waits patiently by the door until someone finally takes pity on him.

The crowning moment of this Christmas came at Party Headquarters, the breathtaking palace where the brother-in-law worked.

Every morning, they would go to the vast circular market in the misty stadium, an eye of snow and sorrow. Here, thieves and paupers gathered to sell looted icons, tins of caviar, Russian uniforms and ridiculous, pathetic knick-knacks to compassionate souls. But a handful of wily merchants had already begun to make fortunes like genuine Western criminals. The market was a dangerous place, according to the wife. Everywhere in Warsaw was dangerous if she was to be believed. Even the cemetery where her mother was buried – the largest cemetery in Europe – was a forest teeming with velvet-fingered thieves. The workmen who built it are buried near the gates, beside the wooden chapel. They had visited the cemetery the night before. It was already dark. Millions of candles flickered on gravestones. It was breathtaking. The uncle kept a lookout for unlikely thieves lurking behind shadowy trees. In this vast cemetery, his nervous wife could not find her mother's grave. A victim of cancer, her mother had died at fifty-eight behind a screen in a seedy hospital. The wife had bought the tattered screen from one of the doctors. Now she could not even find the grave any more. The uncle wished he had known the mother, if only so that he could have solemnly promised, in a desperate, dog-like voice, that he would make her daughter happy. Happiness was something the mother had seen little of in fifty years of communism. She had opened her eyes for a moment, stared at the shadowy Vistula, and died. With snow in her heart. With the hazy memory of lakes in July when she would go to Mazuria with her daughters.

Here in the stadium market, a meeting point for devious traders and wretched peoples from far beyond Poland's borders, surrounded by worthless objects – wooden egg cups, plastic salad bowls and pitiful saucepans, by cut-price heirlooms, astrakhan coats and Russian icons – the millionaire uncle smelled a bargain. He rediscovered the primitive, jubilant soul of his inner haggler. He was not the only one. Shabby tourists haggled over tins of caviar, carried off icons. He bought a fox fur hat from some slant-eyed Russians for a hundred francs – three hundred thousand zlotys – a fortune. He only wore it once, one evening when some drunken Pole shouted 'Tartar whore' at him. He stood staring at the stadium full of Russian guns and uniforms. Suddenly, the uncle, the child of stern civil servants, felt the urge to set up his own business. He would start a fashion for Russian medals, the innumerable multicoloured rows of decorations worn by the Soviet military. He would flood the French market with women's ready-to-wear. The laws of commerce are usually simple: all you need is a rich country and a poor country. The wife listened distractedly, the medals brought back terrible memories. In the end, she agreed to wear one as a brooch on her jacket.

And so they entered the palace of the free market on New Year's Eve, the magnificent redhead wearing her provocative medal, the uncle looking half-Jewish. Disapproval flickered over the faces of the other guests. It was quite shocking to see a daughter of undying Poland wearing a symbol of the oppressor, married to a man who looked like something that had escaped from a Polish zoo. But the brother-in-law knew how to smooth things over. The Minister of Defence warmly shook hands with them, after which the uncle was free to gambol off in search of many drinks. On the terraces of the palace he chatted to beautiful Polish women enamoured of France. Midnight came. Everyone went out onto the balcony overlooking the inexorable snow. It was −20°. The uncle was sweating among all these cheerful people. It was a real New Year's Eve with a fireworks display in a country that could stand tall again. Everyone brandished a glass or a bottle and kissed each other on the lips under the designer sky. They had struggled and survived. There was real joy, and a nostalgia for the years of struggle. The uncle found the tall, red-haired beauty. They kissed for a long time, momentarily oblivious to the fact that they probably did not actually love each other.

The following year, the uncle went back to Warsaw, but things were not the same. In the space of a year, thriving businesses had already sprung up, there were more cars and more expensive models. The sense of magical wonder had vanished.

Every year since then investors have probably made great strides over there. The uncle imagines people out for an evening stroll sporting mobile phones. Poland is about to join the European Union. Only the snow remains.

X

Let us take a closer look at an emotional suicide attempt.

A wedding is a joyous occasion. The French Republic actively helps you with your preparations. It shares in your joy. Its bureaucracy displays an unusual, almost euphoric lightness of touch. In actual fact, to the State, the partners are simply rabbits about to procreate and perpetuate social harmony. Getting married is the easiest thing in the world. A few quick, cheap, routine formalities. In less than a month, it is done and dusted. This surprising straightforwardness is very different from the long-winded, leaden and expensive process of divorce which will inevitably follow. Of course, it is always easier to take out a subscription than to cancel it. Marriage – a subscription of indeterminate duration – is no exception. It is a product the State sells off cheap on summer days and only very reluctantly refunds.

The *livret de famille* is a handsome object with a cover soft as velvet. The layout of the book gives it an undeniable gravity, with its blank death certificates to be filled out for husband, wife and up to eight children. A *livret de famille* can be summarized by two key formulae: 'The bride and groom have declared their desire to take one another as their wedded spouse and we, in the name of the law, have pronounced them to be joined in marriage' and 'Marriage dissolved by divorce granted on the . . .' The second of these is much less impressive than the first; it takes only an official stamp affixed with exacting precision by some depressed local authority worker. Local authority workers are usually bachelors, old maids or special needs persons making up the government quota. There are obviously only two criteria for being hired: apathy and elegant handwriting. This happy breed spends eight hours a day working in an office full of stunted plants. There are probably cruel but imperceptible power struggles. Of all local government offices, the registry office is the most entertaining. Here, a partition separates one desk from all the others. If you felt inclined, you might go there to register a death or two. The possibility of making a mistake – registering a death at the births window or vice versa – is obviously negligible and probably happens rarely. The partition, however, is no guarantee of confidentiality. You might be there registering Noémie's death with quiet dignity while some overexcited father is trumpeting the news of little Kevin's birth on the other side of the partition. It is infuriating. Beware partitions. Take peep shows, for example. Registry offices and peep shows have nothing in common except the partition problem. In peep shows, the private cubicles are all lined up next to one another. The partitions separating them are very thin. They are more expensive than ordinary peep shows, but more disappointing. A slightly vulgar female employee sits facing you. Each customer has his own. She is chewing gum. There are runs in her stockings. There is a one-way mirror between you. You can talk to her, she can talk to you. The mirror is there to protect your anonymity. But just as you are getting comfortable in your private cabin, she says: 'Hey, aren't you the Jewish guy?' Her vagina is practically under your nose. You strike up a conversation. She has a terrible headache: 'God, I've got such a headache, sweetheart.' You sympathize. She will try to make the effort. She coats two fingers with saliva and mechanically starts to stroke her red-raw vagina. She looks at her watch, chews her gum and carries on an almost worldly conversation: 'So, tell me, sweetheart, what do you do for a living?' she asks, scratching her pubes. You're about to tell her you are a poli-sci student, but your neighbour gets in first. He's a computer programmer, you discover. He lets out a long moan. Your hostess picks up her panties and leaves. Beware partitions.

The uncle's recipe for a successful marriage is foolproof. Meet a depressed Polish girl in June and marry her in September. Any other foreigner will do, as long as she is depressive. You are thirty years old. Breton describes someone he once loved as the most beautiful, most unhappy woman in the world. On that June evening you, too, hit the jackpot: an extraordinarily beautiful girl whose unhappiness is as immeasurable as your own. She is absolutely not your type, of course. You usually prefer slightly vulgar women, women who wear thongs out of desperation, the women who make this world almost bearable, the sort of metaphysical sluts God created late one Saturday night in some seedy dive – for God, like every working man in the world, God, who made man in his own image, probably went out drinking on Saturday night – those girls who struggle with slick, disdainful loins, because more than any other living creature they wanted to remain uncreated.

That June evening, like every other evening on earth, you went out in search of a one-night stand. But at a gallery opening, one of those private viewings best avoided like the plague, you find yourself talking to an aristocratic girl whose beauty is not degenerate. Objectively, you think she is stunning, but she is not your type. Unfortunately, at that moment you cannot know that she is your future wife. But sooner or later in the universe of love random souls meet on planets narrow as lifelines, after long periods of emptiness. The fact that you're at a conceptual art exhibition and that you've drunk seven glasses of champagne might account for the fact that your mind is a blank, here in the vast, deserted Hôtel de Sully where a few of these Poles mingle. You are introduced to the artist, a hulking creature of indeterminate sex. His hair is yellow, making him look like a scarecrow. He says enigmatic things. Spends frequent periods in psychiatric hospitals. What is conceptual art? Does conceptual art exert some influence over mixed marriages, over meetings between lost souls? Or do conceptual art and marriage have nothing in common, like registry offices and peep shows? Let us take a look at a few works of conceptual art . . . Imagine three yellowish-brown rectangles aligned vertically, each of which contains a smaller white rectangle, and inside each white rectangle is a short inscription in the artist's handwriting: 'salted', 'lightly salted', 'unsalted.' Farther along, standing in front of a still life, you knock back your eighth glass of champagne. The still life is a photograph, the background is completely black, you can just make out a plastic dinosaur and three baskets of cherries. All around you people are speaking Polish, your head spins pleasantly in the dizziness of whispered consonants. Now we come to a masterpiece which we will take the liberty of reproducing, since it definitely played a part in the subliminal planning for the uncle's brilliant marriage:

The Hôtel de Sully is vast and gloomy. Enigmatic inscriptions multiply in the dying June light, in the conceptual light of the kneeling month: '*Asparagus may sometimes be BEET*', '*The place might have been a net*', '*The Swiss often tell fireside stories when they're*

amongst themselves' etc. They are clearly portents.
'BEET' for example, is the tetragram of the redoubtable
God. From France and Poland, BEET brought forth
two irreconcilable souls and arranged for them to meet.
But you are blind because you will not see. Your
marriage is imminent. Mysterious Poles pass, and their
smiles are an annunciation. They point you out, talking amongst themselves in low voices. Their wings are
barely hidden beneath their tight, nylon parkas.
Standing by a high window, the tall virginal redhead,
your wife-to-be, the woman without a thong gives you
a mocking, enigmatic smile and asks: 'Do you like the
exhibition?' But you reply: 'Who is BEET? Did BEET
send you?' – with the holy terror of a sexual waste-
land foretold. She pretends not to understand. She
takes her seraphic vice as far as turning her back when
you shout: 'So you are BEET!' And you can no longer
see her hair, the dazzling rain of carrots in which mocking cherubs swim. She is staring at what seems to be
the centrepiece in the exhibition now. It is obviously a
conceptual crucifixion. Seven orange panels are aligned
horizontally, surmounted by a large orange square
containing a black circle. This black circle is obviously
a representation of BEET, the god of inescapable
marriages. In each of the seven rectangles, the same
word is repeated: 'doomed'. You still have time to
escape. Didn't you see some depraved brunette, a thong-
wearer, a non-conceptual triangle somewhere at this
Night of the Galleries? – because on this June evening

all of these holy places keep watch in this city of master-works. You still have time to escape. To run towards a vagina of disorder and ammonia. A reserve vagina, a standby, a spare. A merciful, no-obligation, cornu-copia of a vagina. But you stand beside this honeyed angel and look at the crucifixion, repeating over and over in a cosmic fit of giggles: 'Seven times doomed! Seven times doomed!' – while the Poles flutter about in a hum of downy consonants on this night of attempted marriage.

On balance you would have to admit that this marriage was in some sense your salvation, your one act of faith in an otherwise secular life, the sort of ecstatic, slightly frenzied act of faith probably common-place among early Christians. A dazzling belief in the good news, in the long line of prophets and plump friars, an act as blissful as sitting down to bacon and eels in the rustic refectory.

That evening you are introduced to the artist, prince and psychotropic drug-eater Eustache the Pole, with his nasal drawl and his self-centred dachshund Peggy (named after Peggy Guggenheim), who has probably joined her namesake in the land of the shades long ago – or perhaps not yet – barking beneath the tightly packed folds of the earth, in the motherlode of things that will never return, unless through contrite hearts, for it is only posthumously that we come to love that which we lack, our ruined fathers. But that night Eustache, the old Pole, is full of life and skilful evasions.

You are honoured, as you stand there in your square-toed shoes, 'so they take up less room in the box', *you say.*

You also meet his wife Anka, an avant-garde gallery owner whose first husband, a Polish prince, drinks vodka and milk alternately from the moment he wakes up and traces conceptual blue lines on white walls, a negative image of the skywriting of aeroplanes.

You were introduced to an endless stream of Polish deviants.

Then the Hôtel de Sully closed its doors.

And so everyone headed out for a supplementary drinking binge – the scarecrow, the self-centred dachshund, the woman without a thong, the uncle, prince Eustache, countess Anka, a number of unknown Poles, and countless glasses of champagne, in an endless taxi driven by one of the emissaries of BEET – for who but a celestial coachman would have allowed this braying throng into his car? Someone laughed and suggested the uncle would be doing Poland a favour if he married the woman without a thong. It was a joke, of course. He parried it with considerable grace. He turned to the woman and, in typical French fashion, quipped: 'Just name the day!' The day came three months later.

In linguistics, 'performatives' are words or phrases that, when spoken, perform the act or create the state of affairs to which they refer. 'I now pronounce you man and wife' is a performative. The uncle's quip might be regarded as something similar. Admittedly at the time neither he, nor his bride, nor his thirsty witnesses were aware of its effect. All the same, it seems obvious that the uncle *performed* his own wedding in a taxi full of laughing Poles heading towards Bastille. The rest is mere formality. Or, if you prefer, 'The rest is irony, long, weary waiting for death', as Bataille wrote in *Madame Edwarda* – which, it should be noted, also ends in a taxi.

The summer of 1990 is unusually hot and plays an important role in this burgeoning passion, making it seem extraordinary, almost apocalyptic. The god BEET continues to watch over your forthcoming union. You buy spray bottles of chilled water and regularly go out at night. Your Western middle-manager's salary magically provides an endless stream of stunning gifts and trips. Your future wife is disorientated. She thought she was only in France for the summer to earn a little money, and your gallant quip in back of the taxi has already faded into the distance. Four months earlier, her mother had died. This is why she left Poland. Like you, her life is on hold, in the sort of no-man's-land receptive to passionate quirks of fate.

She spends July looking after a wealthy invalid among the Normandy cattle and sends you one or two letters. In August, she comes back to Paris.

Things begin to get serious. The capital is deserted. You suggest she come and stay at your place until she leaves, which she is due to do the following month. Your three-room apartment in Barbès is stylishly sandwiched between the Rue des Drogués and the Rue des Tissus Africains. 'There are lots of blacks', Jojo remarks – Jojo is your future wife's name. It is true that, *this year*, the blacks have not gone away for the holidays, preferring to hang out in gangs of twenty or so, laughing and frolicking on the pavements late into the night. Barbès is completely different from Warsaw. Warsaw is where the only black man in Poland lives. You met him on Christmas Day, standing in the middle of a huge square. He was lost. 'Yeah . . .' you reply, 'but did you realize that you're living in one of the most famous districts in Europe for weaving djellabas? The African diplomats' wives flock here, swaying and oiled like so many . . .'. 'There are lots of Arabs, too', Jojo murmurs. 'I know! Just look at them strutting around in their baggy pyjamas! And, you know what? There are no Jews . . .' you mention slyly, *just in case*.

Shopping for groceries is a mystical act vital to the development of a relationship. So, your first guided tour of the neighbourhood is to the local Monoprix – a trip that will haunt you through your long and melancholy odyssey. It is a proper Monoprix split over two floors and passably chic. The uncle has always loved Monoprix; it brings out the five-year-old boy in him. Shopping is the poor man's weekly Christmas, the balm that brings couples together. And so, on the first day of August, when she has just arrived back from Normandy, you feverishly summon Jojo to Canaan: 'Come on, Jojo, let us venture to the far bank of the river, to the prepackaged herds!' She is beautiful and pale as the exiled ghost. You barely reach the first aisle when she has a panic attack and wants to leave. After all, she is a Polish woman suddenly confronted with the icons of the West – the multicoloured, polytheistic, superfluous West. You explain to her that there is a god of cornflakes who is worshipped under seven or eight different brand names but that they are one and the same god, whose common name is 'Monopolsk', a name whispered only in dread . . . She says a little cruelly: 'You don't eat the cornflakes, the cornflakes eat you!' Because it taunts her, this childish packaging designed by moronic companies, by brainless executives who will soon die of cancer, this vast panoply of a Western civilisation barely less corrupt than its Eastern counterpart, it taunts her from the kilometres of shelves. 'It's like a morgue,' she says, 'and you know, you're all arseholes,' she goes on, 'with your almost-top-of-the-range cars and your shadowless minds, so stop trying to wind me up with your Monoprix, you little French shit!' You catch up with her on the Rue Marx-Dormoy; she is in tears. She trembles in your arms for a long time. Her shoulders pale and angry. She smells of blood and of silken cheeks, like all victims robbed of words.

You get married in September. The reception at your parents' house is as naive as the art movement that bears its name. It is like a kid's birthday party. Disappointed, your new wife keeps to herself. You promise her you will have a proper, formal celebration later. 'A wedding banquet', you explain joyfully. Of your union, a cat is born. The creature appears in your apartment exactly nine months after the wedding. All procreating couples respect nature's cycle. You name it Chopin. You picked out the cat yourself at an SPCA refuge one aimless Saturday. Your wife had always lived with animals, whose silence and suffering mirrored her own. And so, in an attempt to heal the sadness of her exile, you conceived the company of a cat. You even went so far as to choose a son who resembled his mother. Like her, Chopin was born in August, someone at the SPCA tells you over the agonised yelping. He is the youngest kitten in the refuge. He is gentle and timorous. He is ginger. At night he runs wild, shaking his little bell.

In the evenings, you drink heavily. Your wife has started therapy. Her psychoanalyst is obviously well adjusted. She spends six months of the year on holiday, and during consultations at her office near the Bois de Vincennes she spends her time making clever puns. For example, Jojo tells her, 'I have a burning pain when I wee'. Her psychoanalyst joyously repeats: 'I/We! I/We! I/WE!' She repeats this three times in case Jojo did not get it the first time. Jojo is ecstatic. That night over dinner she announces: 'I/WE!' Her depression is in good hands. Psychoanalysts are a public convenience: they're the sewers where grievances are dumped. Basically, you shit on them rather than on your nearest and dearest.

Psychoanalysts are covered in shit but smile enigmatically. Your nearest and dearest are very happy. Everyone knows that psychoanalysts do not tout for business. Even so, you wind up visiting a local disciple of Lacan. In an apparent attempt to save your marriage. Your therapist is pleasant and completely useless. For a whole year, Social Security pays for your evasive replies, your *denial*, and your polite small talk, since it turns out that he is a public health psychoanalyst. He is extremely proficient. At the very first session you tell him that you write. He is overjoyed: 'Right! Right! RIGHT!' He also repeats things three times, as if the word were a bell intended to alert you to some fundamental discovery. At the very next session, you try the *'I wee'* schtick. It works pretty well. The miracle of analysis happens in the first month, the rest is farce. The weaker and more gullible you are, the longer the farce. But that first month enables you to make several crucial life changes. You no longer drink a bottle of whisky every night, for example; instead you drink three litres of beer. It is a form of transference. Psychoanalysis teaches you one vital lesson: it teaches you that seeing a psychoanalyst is pointless, that we are all responsible for sorting out our own shit. This is no minor breakthrough.

You live together for four years. In the last six months, you no longer sleep with your *sister*. You make a vague attempt to be unfaithful but wimp out at the last minute. Eventually, she will leave you because you cannot summon the courage to do it. You help her move her stuff out. She helps you. You divide up the chattels of the marriage between you. After the breakup, you often drop by her place. Now and then, you sleep over. In fact, it will be another four years before you completely separate. Every fortnight, you take Chopin over to her place. It is a minor heartbreak, but you agreed to joint custody of the cat.

Family court judges witness strange things. On a beautiful autumn morning, Jojo, gargantuan Jojo, radiant Jojo sits enthroned in an armchair. She is seven months pregnant. Not by you, obviously, given that you have been separated for two years. The judge, a gentle, kindly man, pronounces the decree absolute and ventures to hope that each of you will soon find happiness in a new union with a *more appropriate partner.* Those are his exact words. Jojo giggles. You giggle too, and pat her swollen belly. The judge shakes hands with both of you. After the ceremony, you have coffee with Jojo by the Seine. You are still good friends. But the atmosphere today is nostalgic. Soon the bus will carry her off along the river wherein our love flows etc. Don't worry: you will see her again. She got pregnant by a man she had a casual fling with. He is married, a family man. He wants nothing to do with a bastard. This means you will soon be left holding the baby.

Your adorable family is panic-stricken. Your mother phones you at least five times a day: 'Watch yourself! She is going to saddle you with looking after that child!' The mammals always put in an appearance during a crisis. They have your geostrategic interests at heart. When you first separated, for example, they advised you not to *abandon* the washing machine. The aforesaid washing machine – a state-of-the-art Siemens – was a wedding present. The mammals chose it after lengthy and painstaking market research. They signed up for a five-year extended warranty. During your breakup they remind you of this fact: 'I hope you're not going to let her keep the Siemens with the five-year extended warranty!' But that is precisely what you do. The high opinion your family has of Poles, especially Polish women, reaches its apogee.

And yet today, as the bus takes her far away, you feel strange and sad. Jojo, too, must be feeling strange. The only stability she has now, the one thing left in this country of exile that has not been ruined, is inside her.

If she had been French, you probably would never have married her. You would have lived together for a couple of months, *and that would have been the end of the story*. But marrying her was the easiest way for her to stay in France. Besides, after your endless romantic peregrinations you wanted to get married. Marriage was something exotic, it was a challenge. And, as if to emphasize its exoticism, you needed to marry a Polish woman, someone who had lived on the far side of the Iron Curtain. But you wanted something else, too; you wanted to save her. From her sadness. From her uncommercial beauty. From her overweening pride.

Because you loved her – and rest assured, you did love her – but, as ever, this is something you didn't realize until it was too late. You were two lost children in the shadow of the infantile architecture of Montmartre. As night fell and streets quivered in the little lights, it was cold inside all the love in the world. You loved her pride, her gentleness, her exile. Her sadness like a cloud. Her wild, ungovernable sadness. And tonight, you are tortured by dreams in which you see her on a Warsaw street. She is on her way home from work. She is going to pick up her son. She walks across the snow in the antiquated light of Warsaw, and you hope that she is happy, for as long as she is not happy you can never truly be at peace.

XI

Now we come to the period you spend passionately hanging out in the nightclubs of Pigalle. You are unemployed. Social Security is only too happy to finance such small-scale breakdowns. Clubs, as everyone knows, can be divided into three categories, the most important two being nightclubs and *afters*. *Befores* are reserved mainly for a very small, very wounded clientèle. The nightclub community, like all communities, is a closed world: you run into the same people wherever you go. It is a community drawn from a broad spectrum of the walking wounded, specifically the professional nighthawks: waitresses, barmen, doormen, regulars of particular bars and clubs, hostesses from strip clubs who have come to chill out, teenage girls on the verge of prostitution, well-hung black dancers in search of a social acceptance they will never find anywhere else, transvestites, transsexuals, etc. You start off in a bar sometime around midnight, move on to a club, then another bar, then an *after*, then a few more bars, then a *before*, then bed. In the last of these places you're usually alone. It is 5:00 p.m. It is an exciting, completely fulfilling life. At 6 a.m., nightclubs smell of liver failure. As indeed do you, although you're convinced that you exude a sweet scent made up of champagne, scotch and coke, gin and tonic, tequila, rum, mescal, etc. You have drunk all the blue liqueur from all the lagoons in the world. Some people claim that leaving an *after* at noon in the middle of summer is a glorious experience, you feel light spilling onto your face, you are serene and sated with pleasure. This is a lie. You stagger home, you're wearing sunglasses partly to protect you from death by radiation but also so people won't see the bags under your eyes. Nighthawks always wear dark glasses. A terrifying world, a world you're no longer part of, bustles all around you. The uncle often wakes up in deserted parks alone and tachycardic. It is 7 a.m. As soon as he gets home, he calls his friends. He tells them life is as thrilling as a shock of nervous energy and that he doesn't feel the need to sleep much any more. These conversations are usually brief. His friends are only just awake and are heading out to work. They quickly hang up. So the uncle listens to the healing organ, the convivial organ, of Widor's sweet, savage *Symphonie Gothique* and starts to write. Charles-Marie Widor stares out from the CD cover like a stern grandfather. From the depths of the nineteenth century, he seems to judge the uncle and find him sorely wanting. So the uncle portentously addresses him. The greatness of your art, Charles-Marie, is that you can console an alcoholic at seven o'clock in the morning, someone who has drunk half the sorrows of the world and who is still thirsty. While others were carousing, you spent your evenings with herbal tea and belfries composing music to caress our souls. The organ whispers like the one true consoling love. The organ exudes the ephemeral scent of a woman, lays its ethereal hands upon your ailing temples, as the waitress at the last bar you visited might have done if you hadn't preferred liquor to love, if you hadn't slipped silently into the depths of your wound.

Who is Linda? The uncle has just walked her home through the pale, toxic dawn to the locked shutters of a sex shop. Garbage trucks are taking away the rubbish and the cans. Linda is twenty and has already experienced the incomparable joy, the great nervous laughter, of despair. Linda lives with her sister and her brother-in-law who run a sex shop in Pigalle. That is her story. Every night she goes clubbing at the Moloko. She and the uncle often have a chat. To her, the uncle represents a sort of father figure groping in the grim moral darkness, his penis standing proudly to attention at the prospect of some impossible incest. Linda is constantly popping pills. The uncle warns her to be careful. In one night, laughingly, recklessly, she might sleep with three men. The dawn is romantic, desolate. Linda disappears under the iron curtain of the sex shop. The uncle heads home with his troublesome friend, alcohol, which lies like an unripe fruit in his stomach, like an endless youth that only death will relieve. Because you have no intention of giving up on this outstanding, foetal failure. On this failure to which you have not found the key. On this hidden door that is yourself. On this conflicted carcass of misery and jubilation. On this pointless golden rain. On these clichéd bar-room conversations that take the place of love. On this insistent desire to fall asleep forever. On this pitched battle between the dragon and the rational. On this disillusioned dawn. On the ordeal of youth, the paradises endlessly putting up the shutters. On this murky communion wine. On the transubstantiation of the body of the mother.

Going home alone in the defeat that is the dawn is a terrible thing because it is both misery and an immense happiness. There is no woman walking beside you. No stumbling wretch, no brilliant contender determined to save you, no twenty-year-old shooting star materializing from who knows where. But you wouldn't swap this for a structured, safe, comfortable life. You're happy because the order of things is turned on its head. You're locked in constant battle with this life that was given to you against your will, and in this pallid end-game you finally feel you have earned the right to destroy yourself.

Then there is Francine. Francine presides over the toilets. She is one of the cornerstones of the Moloko. She sits enthroned on the first floor where she has her court, her allies, her retinue. The uncle spends whole evenings chatting to her about everything and nothing, about the froth of the everyday, unemployment, about the girls who dance and move on, about loneliness. Together in the midst of the dark velvet, Francine and the uncle make up an ephemeral, fraternal couple. He buys her drinks, gives her a neck rub when she is tired at the end of the night. She is fifty and a typical Parisian, with her working-class vernacular and her accent. She used to work in catering. She will retire somewhere in the Camargue. She rules over the toilets – a strategic hub, part medical centre, the intersection for love affairs, and ideally placed if there is any scandal – with a firm, derisive hand. She calls the girls 'little twats'. She knows who's who and what's what: 'Would you look at the state of that little twat?' Honestly, it's a disgrace!' She knows Linda and does her best to keep an eye on her. Francine and the uncle talk about Linda as if she were a slightly kooky younger sister, a heartbreaking wonder.

Then there is the man who sells roses, a plump man who always wears a jacket. He's not like the other rose-sellers, he's long since given up traipsing through restaurants. He seems to be quite well off. Every year he takes his wife and family back to India. Every night he sells his wares at the Moloko like an unwearied fisher of souls. Sometimes, he sits and has a drink in the middle of the throng. Or takes a run on the dance floor with his huge bouquet of flowers. He's happy. He shakes hands with the regulars, always with the same amused comments: 'Many pretty girls tonight!'. Sooner or later, he knows, people will come to him to buy evanescent roses which will wind up in gutters or next to the dim mirrors of unknown girls.

There is a poem by Malcolm Lowry called 'Thirty-Five Mescals at Cuantla'. Sometimes the uncle makes an inventory of everything he has drunk in the course of some excessive evening: two and a half pints of beer, a bottle of white wine, another pint of beer, two shots of some exotic spirit, a glass of punch, half a pint of beer, a glass of white wine, three scotch and cokes. After that, everything becomes magnificently vague: blue cocktails of champagne and curaçao served in tall glasses which come with names that are bitter and break like waves, glass after glass of gin, coffee liqueurs, liqueurs dispensed from bottles where scorpions and snakes intertwine. And you can never have enough. Because the *thing* demands more, this bottomless thing into which you must constantly pour more alcohol. This thing that tolerates no restrictions. Violent and tragic. Jubilant. Its jubilation measureless and deadly. This thing that sends out troops to whip up reinforcements from far-off muscles. It is a thing erect. Its eyes wide. Still on its feet at 3 a.m., at 6 a.m. This thing dancing on the edge of an abyss with infinite sadness. But a sadness transformed into strength. This thing that, despite the tragedy, is still prepared to gamble on love. This man.

And then there is the *after* near the Place Clichy. Here the uncle meets transsexuals drowning their sorrows in the tormented light while everywhere families are waking and dreams are guttering out. There is no beauty more heartbreaking, more hopeless, than that of the transsexual. The uncle wrote a short piece about it back when he used to hang out with them, and he wouldn't phrase it any differently today . . .

The terrible heat of July mornings when I saw the angel at the smithy of the after! *Angel eyes! So pale! I need to see them every day, those burned out, beaten eyes. Those eyes which seek only love, in which at a glance you can read – with no attempt to judge or condemn – the full scope of love from its lowest depths to its loftiest heights . . . And I knew, I knew without judging on the first morning we met, starving and unfulfilled, that this angel with an irradiated glance could have seized my penis through the cloth . . . But were they really her eyes, her long blonde hair, her cold heavy breasts, when by midday, in the midst of desperate kisses, I could feel the unchangeable sign of his sex reappear on her cheeks?*

'Dance! Dance for me!' the angel begged in a hoarse voice. He bit my lips. Alcohol burned my shoulders. Wings ripped my flesh in these decadent hours of excess. 'Dance for me!' . . . Oh, how hoarse her voice was. She lifted her skirt and made a wanking gesture or was she trying to show me, as I turned away, that there was nothing left but a mass of useless flesh, a permanent zipper which

cut her off forever from the possibility of love?
And so I danced, with terrible pain and terrible
joy. My shoes split, the skin on my feet flayed raw,
all through that fiery month in the most exquisite
hell I have ever known. The angel's eyes followed
this loveless dance, this fire, this suffering, which
eventually left me in tears, in the half-light, on the
last empty sofa.

I met ulcerated, unhappy, destitute creatures.
The kissing came to a sudden end. Oh, people of
the dawn! We insulted one another on the pave-
ments, in front of poker-faced doormen – those
solid monsters sculpted in the doorways, standing
guard over the Gates of Excess, insensitive to our
pain. The alcohol was endless. Soon, we would
have no money, no words, only a desperate need
to come back again . . .

Then comes the reckoning. Clubbing every night is an
expensive business. You enthusiastically buy drinks for
every social reject. Every night, you make several trips
to the ATM. You don't dare check your balance any
more. Your redundancy money has long since been squan-
dered. ATMs glitter in the night like shrines calling to
you. Even during the day, you feel a shudder every time
you pass one. ATMs are whores and tomorrow night
they will turn you on again, with the painted smile of
oblivion. You dance on life's raw nerve. You are danger-
ously happy. A gambler can get himself barred from a

casino: he is free to turn himself in at a police station to negotiate the duration of his exile. You have no such freedom. So, one day, you take a pair of scissors and cut up your ATM card. From now on you will use your chequebook. There follows a bizarre week during which you can't even buy a box of matches and you're reduced to lighting your few last cigarettes on the kitchen stove. You barter with your next-door neighbour, a handsome woman of about fifty you once slept with – thank God – you swap a novel for a little hard cash. You have lots of books and she is only too happy to play mother of tragedy. A couple of days later, you crudely tape your ATM card back together and take out some ready cash. And the nights begin again, amid *the walking wounded who drink theological spirits,* until morning comes and the ATM swallows your card and beckons you back to reality.

II

Bankruptcy

XII

Work is one of the principal causes of human misery, the other is love.

The preamble to the Constitution of the Fourth Republic, still in effect, states 'Everyone shall have the duty to work and the right to obtain employment'. Luckily, unemployment turned up to challenge this hypocrisy.

A handful of arseholes terrorize the whole planet through work. The worst offenders are the people who have no financial or political motive. Intense feelings of frustration turn them into workaholics and they can't bear people who aren't like them. This is a phenomenon that affects every level of humanity. Listen to a Portuguese foreman yelling from a scaffolding rig: he is a vicious, uncultivated animal, and the world would be a better place if someone pushed him off.

The uncle's first bout of depression coincided with his military service. There were probably other contributing factors, but the fact is that his symptoms disappeared as soon as the farce was over.

The Museum on which the uncle *embarked* – these

were the words used in his posting – is attached to the Ministry of Defence. This means it is run by a valiant officer whose wife spends her time feverishly organizing cocktail parties. They live in a two hundred square metre pigsty over the museum. Every Wednesday, the officer summons his closest colleagues: an alcoholic admiral, the curator, the concierge, etc. Everyone carries a briefcase. The agenda for the meeting usually concerns a Commandant Cousteau exhibition or moving a display case. 'Nothing can be created' is the Museum's motto, so exhibits are constantly being moved around. The officer's handshake is very limp.

The Museum is peopled by ex-officers and civilians. The lowest of the low in this hierarchy are the young people from good families. Because they should feel privileged to hole up in a nice museum where the duties are not taxing and you're ordered around by a bunch of fuck-ups. The uncle was posted to Studies and Research, a department famous for its intellectual ferment. He worked as a warehouseman, for a 'salary' of about four hundred francs a month. He also licked envelopes. He learned to let things slide.

The Museum curator is a former quartermaster. He is quite clearly unqualified for his role. He is sixty years old, dyes his hair yellow and wears a bomber jacket. He sailed the seven seas, stopping off at exotic ports. From this he acquired his store of life experience. He teaches the sailors that a Sea Cock is not just a hull valve, it's a state of mind. He has a number of responsibilities:

peddling rumours about the staff, humiliating the weak, knocking back a crafty drink whenever possible, damaging Museum property, luring sailors into the storeroom. Because Marcel La Redoute is a homosexual. The redoubtable Marcel is always on the lookout for a sailor for some menial task. He might need someone to help clean a display case, for example. The uncle doesn't recoil at such jobs. Being assigned to Marcel is painless. It is a chance to escape the unspeakable boredom. First, you head off to the storeroom to pick up some vague cleaning product. Marcel prattles on endlessly. The Museum is almost empty, apart from a handful of children and a few old people fascinated by the steel freighters and the wooden galleons, glorious masterpieces creaking out of boredom in the silence, like the insomniac ex-navy lunatics who created them. You find out bits of interesting gossip: the head of the Research Department is fucking the new sailor, the security guards spend all their time boozing, etc. The cleaning products are right at the back of the storeroom. You have to move a model ship to get to them. Marcel kicks it out of the way, breaking three masts in the process. 'That'll keep the lazy fuckers in the workshop busy!' he says. Marcel regularly slashes paintings by Joseph Vernet. Joseph Vernet is a fine artist who painted at least fourteen ports, a few shipwrecks, and probably one or two mists at sea. A lot of time is spent restoring his paintings. The display case that needs cleaning is as big as a large aquarium. It is the inside that has to be cleaned. The uncle crawls inside. Marcel is a joker. Marcel locks the display case. Marcel stares at the uncle with a strange twinkle in his eyes. Anyone who has never been locked in a display case has missed out on an educational experience: being reduced to a mere object. It is a small exercise in domination. The uncle's imprisonment lasts about two minutes, which Marcel spends more or less masturbating. All in all, it is quite pervy.

The uncle's depression came on suddenly. Being bawled out every morning at 7:15 by some prick who's just waiting for you to be late, shifting display cases that weigh a tonne only to replace them the following day, taking down Vernets in room A to hang them in room B, carrying piles of chairs and partitions, running up and down stairs to Purgatory a hundred times a day, pretending to classify files on *The Redoubtable, The Fearsome, The Terrible, The Brute, The Fuckwit* or Jean-Yves Cousteau, all these things quickly become exhausting for a delicate mammal of refined tastes. You might make more of an effort if these grey gunboats had names that were more benign: *The Depressive, The Defeatist, The Deserter*, etc. Though not all are complete morons – some have even managed to go to university – the military are a crude lot. They form a transitional species between chimpanzee and dolphin. But a world made up principally of men cannot but be crude and dangerous.

The symptoms of your depression get on everyone's nerves. The head of the Research Department, Ms Turpentine, tells the uncle he's a whisker away from being fired. His connections won't save him. There are scores of other seamen who dream of *embarking* on the tempestuous raft of the Museum. Ms Turpentine is the daughter of a family of naval officers. Physically, she is of no interest whatsoever. She spends all day sulking. Because she has a degree in something or other, she despises the uncle. The uncle thinks she is lesbian. Marcel La Redoute, on the other hand, thinks all the bitch needs is a good seeing to. In fact, he tells you in the secret storerooms, she is being fucked rigid by the new sailor. The new sailor has been assigned to the Friends of the Museum. The main responsibility of the Friends of the Museum is selling key-rings. Godefroy is some sort of village squire; he has an aristocratic name, in any case. Everyone on the raft is terribly deferential. But, Marcel explains, he's not from one of the great French aristocratic families. Because a true aristocratic French family knows how to keep tradition alive, churning out courtesans and incompetents. Every family has its speciality. Some specialize in miscarriages. In Marcel's opinion, Godefroy is nothing more than an ass-licker. He's been *indulging in sodomy* with Turpentine in the hope of getting a job as a lecturer. You think there is probably something in what Marcel says: Godefroy is tall, nearly two hundred centimetres, offhand, well adjusted and enjoys rock-climbing; he's a devious moron with not much of a future, unless it is to procreate with Turpentine and give lectures about tuna fishing.

The Research Department is a storehouse of books, index cards and photocopies, and is mostly frequented by two or three pensioners who spend hours looking at old photographs. An escort vessel slicing through the waters of the Gulf of Siam with the harbour in the distance. The pensioners make notes. They're preparing important publications on life aboard escort vessels. The librarian's job is to meet with these old codgers and answer their fanatical letters. The most pitiful loser in the Research Department is a man with a little grey moustache, someone who immediately warmed to the uncle, seeing in him an ally. In fact, everyone despises Passereau. He is the only man in the department. He is fifty years old. His mediocrity cruelly mirrors that of his co-workers. Turpentine would dearly love to fire him. Passereau is a civilian. He's never been to sea. It is the great tragedy of his life. His trivial knowledge is irritating. For example, he knows the dates on which construction began on every single ship. Passereau has a wife and a son. The family lives in a tragicomic three-room apartment at La Kremlin-Bicêtre. He has lunch in the navy barracks mess. He rolls back to the office a little tipsy. Every afternoon he phones his wife for an update on the evening menu. When the bell rings at five o'clock, Passereau slips on his raincoat with a graceful smile, a smile that masks his failure. The uncle was rather fond of Passereau.

Every two years, the Museum becomes a hive of activity as it organizes a perilous avant-garde event:

the Navy Fair. Crude daubs reminiscent of Soviet art are entered in competition. A jury confers a prestigious title, which the laureate is entitled to use for the rest of his life. He can have it printed on his business card: 'Yvon Coitus, artist by appointment to the Navy.' Challenging works of art are exhibited at the Museum: *Escort Vessel in the Mist, Rain Over the Lann-Bihoué Naval Air Station, Kelp at Pleumeur-Bodou,* etc.

Seven hundred and fifty Lexomil later, the uncle was free. That very day or almost, his depression vanished. The lead and dust in his blood became as gold, albeit a somewhat tarnished gold. This first experience of working life stamped on his flesh the knowledge of his own mortality.

In the 1970s, France gave birth to a minor technological revolution, a text-based forerunner of the world wide web: *le Minitel.* In the 1980s, commercial uses for this technology proliferated. Newspaper groups were the first to make a killing. With Minitel, they made good their losses in more traditional media. Then the Internet came along to supplant this radical invention.

We will call the newspaper group the uncle worked for 'Bagatel'. As far as the Minitel was concerned, he could not have chosen better: Bagatel was *le leader.*

The first time the uncle heard the word 'product' he felt like throwing up. In business, people use it constantly. Within a week, you find yourself using the word with a pathetic, hysterical pleasure. You start spending more and more time at the office. You have become a product.

The managing editor of Bagatel used to be a secretary. The company is carefully exploring this new technology and feels no need to hire a ruinously expensive graduate. Monique jumped at the chance. She is single and anorexic. She has the figure of a prepubescent girl. At lunch, she eats some salad-like substance with a disgusted moue. She works a sixteen-hour day. Her hobbies are limited to mass on Sunday and her nephews. She phones her employees at home at all hours of the day and night. Like all managers, she prefers employees who are single and, if possible, anorexic. Monique has nothing against love affairs as long as they take place within the department. When the uncle falls for a twenty-year-old journalist, Monique proffers the understatement: 'I've nothing against office affairs!' She even goes so far as to say, with a slight smile, 'I knew you'd like her!' Because the more completely the company nurtures your development, the more completely she can count on your devotion. In-house fucking increases productivity. At Les Oreillons, for example, fucking is company policy. In fact, they organize tropical holidays. To motivate the workforce, Monique hires young, beautiful people. This is a brilliant stratagem. Beauty is priceless. Youth is cheap. Everyone is happy.

The senior editor arrives every morning at about ten with an Irish setter. The setter is somewhat stupid, its master somewhat less so. Alexandre is an ambassador's son. He wears a Mac Douglas jacket and is waiting on a considerable inheritance. He dreams of working in television. He is moderately spineless. Still, Alexandre has style. In the uncle he recognized the makings of a perfect assistant. The uncle has lots of ideas and no ambition. So, while the uncle is busy having lots of ideas and no ambition, Alexandre keeps a watchful eye on what the other executives are up to. When Monique goes on holiday, he meets with the Director General. Because a manager must safeguard his position or try for someone else's. This means he spends half his time scheming. The other half, he spends doing as little as possible. Truth be told, you might say Alexandre does nothing. This is why he needs an assistant. Besides, an assistant is a symbol of power. A person to be taken to important meetings. From what we've said, it is obvious that the role of assistant offers distinct advantages: if you relinquish any claim on your boss's job, your boss turns a blind eye to your offhand manner or your incompetence, which are simply a mirror image of his own. Between the two of you, you do the work of a single employee. Things could be worse.

In keeping with these sound principles, much fun was had by all at Bagatel, at least at first.

Every new technology attracts a swarm of carpetbaggers, mostly people without no academic qualifications. This brave new world attracts people to come and try their luck. There is a quasi-bohemian atmosphere. Profit is almost a secondary matter. Later, market forces reassert themselves, competent graduates are hired and the redundancies start.

At Bagatel, the new technology of Minitel was gleefully explored. A little human warmth was brought to bear because, to be honest, there is nothing more bleak than a Minitel screen. They were carving out a user-friendly paradise, an interactive utopia. This was the dawn of a new era in which, everywhere, smiling happy people would eagerly communicate. The apotheosis of this new technology was the chatroom.

In chatrooms, hordes of sexually frustrated idiots assumed sophisticated *nicknames*: 'SWM 10 INCHS SKS SLUT', 'CPL SEEK SEXY F IN THE BURBS', 'LIONESS FOR TEL SEX' etc. Occasionally, you happened on names like 'Isolde' or 'Shy'. Shy's messages, a few sparkling sentences in the darkness, stirred up extraordinary turmoil. She was twenty-five, about 170 centimetres, with green eyes. She worked for France Telecom. A lot of the *nicks* worked for France Telecom. Sooner or later, Shy would tell you that she was wearing nothing but a pair of pink panties and that she was sitting alone in the dark somewhere in Livry-Gargan. This was one of the miracles of Minitel. A bunch of strangers desperate for something real, alone in their concrete huts, had been waiting for true love. Now, suddenly, the night was alive with countless ghostly forms. Undreamed of suburbs began to flicker into life. Everywhere there was loneliness, suffering, deserted ring roads. Mutually, you decided to continue this lyrical, impossible love affair over the phone. Shy was lying on her bed. *I'm lying on my bed!* Your hand stroked her thigh. *I can feel your hand on my thigh!* You ripped off her panties with your teeth. *You're ripping off my panties with your teeth in some ghastly suburb!* After this night of passion, you arranged to meet Shy. Cautiously, you watched, waiting to see what she looked like. You spotted her straight off. She was looking around for someone. She waited for you for a long time. Shy was fifty. She was a little deformed. Gutlessly, you walked off. Chatrooms were like a drug for curing loneliness. Extravagant phone bills and court cases followed – loneliness is a big market. France Telecom, the official pusher, was making a killing.

The uncle was having fun. There is nothing worse than a cool working environment: it is the sort of place where you might lose your soul, assuming you have one. You stay late at the office. You go drinking with your colleagues. You'd probably be better off working in some second-rate hellhole.

Luckily, after the golden age comes the decline. Bagatel lost its place as *le leader*. The atmosphere became tense. No one talked about Utopia any more. They started to talk about trivial things: profits, competition, expansion, etc. The group forced Monique to take on an assistant. She hired her brother. Jean-Charles was an immature wanker from Versailles. He had an MBA of some sort. Like her, he went to mass on Sunday. He was considerably less neurotic than his sister. The management became much stricter. The uncle was requested to actually *manage* his team, prepare budgets, look to the long term. He responded with some puerile sniggering. He lapsed into apathy. He had a screaming match with Monique. It was quietly suggested that he resign. The uncle spent a long time petting the Irish setter. Then he departed this brave new world.

Lots of people bored with their jobs have an extraordinary clothes budget. Let us take Hélène. Hélène is miserable. Her job is a burden. Her love life is little better. If she bought her clothes from the Trois Suisses catalogue, people would assume that, like most people, she is dead inside. Instead, she has exceptional taste in clothes, favouring originals by young, innovative designers. The contrast between her misery and her exaggerated elegance is poignant. She often wears brash colours; in fact she has a coat and hat that are a luminous orange. She looks like a grim motorway pileup.

The uncle had a striking wardrobe when he was working at the science museum at La Villette. He started work there on April 1. The date probably had some bearing on what followed.

During a job interview – as in most human relations – you have approximately thirty seconds to *size up* someone. The risk of making a mistake is generally minimal. People tend to hire others in their own image – real or imagined. Paul La Garenne was prodigiously bored. He was thirty-two. He'd recently been appointed

Department Head, a title he earned through boredom. The interview was tedious. Each recognized in the other an elegant disdain for the world of work. The deal was done.

Even so, Paul was embarrassed when the uncle resigned two weeks later. La Villette is public sector. It takes months to recruit someone. Lots of people have to sign off on a new hire. And so, a slightly surreal phase began on April 15. On the 22nd, the uncle suggested he might work three days a week. 'Just until you find a replacement!' he said cheerfully. Personnel added a codicil to his contract. On May 5, on a whim, the uncle announced just as cheerfully: 'Actually, you know, I will stay!' Paul La Garenne had a facial tic. When nervous, he turned into a rabbit, and the tip of his nose twitched at top speed. A new full-time contract was drawn up. On May 19, the uncle wondered aloud if maybe a four-day week might not be the perfect solution: 'Think about it, Bugs, I'll be less expensive to the company and still calmly able to shoulder my responsibilities.' Paul's ears pricked up. High up in his tower office, the head of personnel was becoming suspicious. There was an endless stream of contracts and codicils. There were rumours about La Garenne. Recent events in his department were worrying. Paul took the lift up to personnel, nervously nibbling on a carrot. He explained to personnel that the uncle was the ideal candidate for the job, and that they had to indulge him in his whims. And so a final contract was drawn up.

Curiously, the uncle was given the job title of engineer. His contract stipulated that he would work four days a week.

If there are emotional suicide attempts, there are also professional suicide attempts. Flaubert, author of *Madame Bovary*, wrote that if you look at it long enough, anything becomes interesting. Flaubert was famous for his long periods of ennui. Seen from a certain lofty vantage point, even a ring road becomes interesting. Every evening, red lights go one way, white lights the other. The red lights are Parisians, the white ones suburbanites. Every morning, the reverse is true. Extraterrestrials who studied us for long enough could not help but notice that we are a species endowed with intelligence. Every evening, a merry band of travellers heads home whistling like the dwarves in *Snow White*. From a tower, it is also possible to see other towers. It is a beautiful sight. The uncle stared out at the view for a long time. In addition to everything else, he suffered from vertigo.

The big guns of Christianity tell us that God bestowed freedom on mankind. Boredom is one of the chief freedoms which God bestowed on man.

The tower block where the uncle works is all offices. It has a pretty name: it is called *Siamese 1*. There is a sister tower next door, *Siamese 2*. There is an overcrowded cafeteria in the basement. The fluorescent lights are savage. Executives wear fake smiles. Lipstick slashes look like open wounds. Complexions are pale. It feels like a nuclear fallout shelter. In fact, it is an architectural disaster. Architecture is a glorious, public, affirmative art that impacts directly on people's everyday lives. Unfortunately, more often than not it is practised by murderers. The architect who designed the Siamese Twins cafeteria made sure that no one would want to hang around: there are concrete benches with a few cushions. Everyone in the place is frantic and smiling. People hurriedly drink their coffee standing up and scuttle back to work. Executives mount an attack on the afternoon. They seem happy enough.

Parking at the Siamese Twins is chockablock. The uncle finally manages to find a parking space, an empty rectangle on some gloomy subterranean level. He adopts it for a few days. Someone leaves notes on his windscreen. The uncle assumes they are flyers and doesn't bother to read them. There are more notes. The third is threatening: 'Don't fuck with me or else!' Suddenly, he feels headlights trained on him. A man emerges from a car. He has clearly been watching and waiting for hours. He's nervous, edgy. He's a spiritless middle-manager, a family man. Someone has stolen his parking spot. For the past week he hasn't been able to sleep, hasn't been able to have sex. His wife's triangle has become a terrifying rectangle. Her clitoris honks like a car horn. The labia majora blink like indicator lights. There could be a gun in the trunk. The uncle apologizes profusely. The uncle seems truly sincere. The uncle didn't understand the laws of the Siamese Twins. It will never happen again! The man is relieved but disappointed. He's been dreaming of corporate spaghetti westerns and car chases. Dreams where he beats up the uncle, reconquers the rectangle, and celebrates his victory inside his geometric wife.

To kill time, the uncle sucks Vichy mints. The Avenue Jean-Jaurès, on the outskirts of Aubervilliers, is nothing special. There are similar rundown houses in the neighbouring streets, hovels made of rusting corrugated iron, remnants. The uncle rather likes these pathetic houses, with their tiny gardens, their orphaned brambles. If he were serious about his life, if he went *all the way*, he'd buy a house here and call it Tahiti or Divine Comedy. He'd have a German shepherd and a couple of suburban cats. He could call the dog Barabbas or Rimbaud. Then he'd have a real life, with a squeaky gate and some low-key cancer. There'd be a little vegetable garden and a little forest, a sort of second childhood before death. Every evening, he'd water the blessed pumpkins as his granddad once did – an old man in a grey smock, stooped and ghostly, pacing the little paths under the furious beaks of the gulls, the thieving gulls in their black balaclavas, still alive, though only just, waiting to join the tubers and the twisting roots in silence and oblivion. Vegetable gardens are metaphysical places. They symbolize self-sufficiency and therefore loneliness. Helpless creatures work there under the aphasic sky. He'd get a new wife, new as new potatoes, a depressed borderline alcoholic. Better still, he'd live alone, utterly alone. The uncle walks very slowly mulling over these thoughts, his eyes vacant. He buys his Vichy mints and climbs his tower. He gets through two packs a day.

The whole department is depressed. Nobody's worried about profitability. The department could function with a staff of three. There are ten of them. But still, Paul seems to have faith, he vaguely negotiates contracts with private companies.

The computer reigns supreme. Fearsome monitors contaminate the soul like a grey, persistent rain. The uncle pretends to work. In his contract it states that he will be a leader of men. He remembers Bagatel, the hazy summer, the twenty-year-old girl he lost one autumn evening. He vaguely goes on writing some book as interminable as his life. He stares out at the ring road. Every now and then he sleeps with one of his young colleagues. She is on a short-term contract and highly motivated. She thinks everyone is incompetent. This is typical. In any company, everyone is suspected of being incompetent. Julie has been working for small, disciplined companies. She understands computer systems perfectly. Her skills and her authority are technical; she has no personality. She yells at the uncle, at Paul and Louis. Louis is head of the IT department. He crashes the system every time he goes near it. Louis comes from one of the oldest families in France. A kind-hearted, balding man, he is incompetent and urbane. He could easily live off the proceeds of his holdings but claims he feels it is his duty to work. It is a noble duty, and one from which everyone would cheerfully agree to exempt him. Louis is president of an association that lobbies in favour of hunting. Hunting is his passion. His arguments are shrewd. The deer has a sporting chance! The wildlife is only slightly decimated! The uncle is quite fond of Louis. Hunting is glamorous. They make conversation. Time passes. Louis passes round his photos, blows his hunting horn in the office, extends invitations to teeming forests, etc. All the while, the system is dying. Programmers are brought in at exorbitant hourly rates to fix it. Louis crashes it again. And on it goes. Louis and Paul are Julie's principal targets. Julie yells at the uncle, but with more affection. He's an incurable poet, a child who writes books.

Then a wave of excitement courses through the Kingdom of the Shades, an unhoped-for resurrection. The department is about to reach the promised land, to merge with Technical Resources. They have crossed the ring road. Far beneath the vast, spherical Imax cinema, the Géode, were the ultra-modern caves of Technical Resources. A light provided the luminous grey glow. Every day, the whole department traipsed across to marvel at their new offices, delirious amid the alien carpets, the whistling builders. They gazed in rapture on their future cages. Getting your own office is a three-day thrill at least. The secretary brought her Louis Vuitton bag and her Hermès scarf. She tested the swivel chairs. You could see her panties and suspenders.

The Science Museum at La Villette faces radiantly towards the future. It has a glass façade, a thousand employees. Most of the people who work there are unbelievably bored. Just like anywhere else. But at La Villette the contrast between the scientific optimism of the place and the abject boredom of the employees is harsher than elsewhere. When the newspaper is no longer enough, when the telephone is no longer enough, when masturbating in the toilets is no longer enough, boredom comes close to suicide. You wander through this godless complex, visit exhibitions about the loathsome cosmos, chat up vacuous women from the PR department. You talk endlessly about how bored you are, a running commentary of pained chuckles. Vast, vast is the land of boredom. Happy is he who struggles against oppression! Happy is the oppressor! Happy is he who will rejoin the sated earth!

XIII

Then came Ubu Publications. This was your crowning achievement, your apotheosis, your apocalypse.

What is a publisher? There is an interesting definition in *Foucault's Pendulum*: a publisher's principal task is to mislay manuscripts. The uncle, who had the privilege of doing just that before he was fired, agrees with Umberto Eco wholeheartedly. However, the definition is incomplete: as well as mislaying manuscripts, a publisher has a duty to leave them in unread piles. It is also a type of comedy in which the bailiffs come in one door as the proprietor nips out the other. The least important cog in the publishing machine is the author. Last but not least, working for a publisher is a privilege, for there you will get to meet the most self-absorbed people on the planet.

The move from La Villette to Ubu Publishing is like a ten thousand-volt shock that jolts you back to life, at least temporarily. You have left a Third World country for a cultural superpower. At last, you feel you have found Paradise, the teeming waters that fish dream of in the spawning season. You feel at home.

Celebrities wander the corridors. There are books, proofs and manuscripts all over the place. Piles of contemporary fiction lie around on the floor. The place is a mess.

Père Ubu weighs in at about 0.12 tonnes. Mère Ubu, maybe 100 grams less. The reception area is decorated with sneering multicoloured skeletons because Père Ubu is obsessed with death. There is a life-sized statue in Mère Ubu's office, nearly two hundred centimetres tall, a statue of the Virgin Mary wearing a lovely white sheet holding an erect phallus. The Mother of God's phallus is about thirty centimetres long. The scene is set.

Ubu Publishing was a child of the 1970s. Like a lot of small publishers back then, it tried to distance itself from the big publishers. Ubu Publishing dares to be different: this is a precept to which everyone at Ubu Publishing defers. In fact, in his office, Père Ubu sings at the top of his voice: 'We defer, we defer all payments!'

Père Ubu is exquisitely neurotic. His thighs quiver on his directorial chair. He smokes two Gauloises at a time. He sweats. He spends all day bellowing at Mère Ubu. Or at his employees. Or both. It all depends how much he's had to drink.

On about the fifteenth of the month everyone at Ubu Publishing gets a little nervous. Employees have strange conversations:

'You get paid yet?'

'No . . . maybe next week, apparently.'

Being paid demands skill. It demands the cunning of Ulysses or Tom Thumb. You might try at around three o'clock, while lunch is settling. You go down to visit Père Ubu in his cavern. Knock knock! 'Who's there?' he thunders. 'Little Red Riding Hood/Tom Thumb/one of your employees, etc.' 'Come in, my child!' Ubu watches as you enter, smiling like a dragon. The ashtray smoulders like a cancerous god. 'I just thought maybe . . .' 'No!' roars this furious barrel of a man. You take off your shirt, show him your protruding ribs: 'Père Ubu! Père Ubu! I beg you! I have bills to pay, *bank charges*, I have to buy beer and cigarettes and my ration of bacon . . .' 'And what about me?' booms Ubu. 'You should consider yourself lucky to have a job at all when times are so hard for me!' He flourishes a sheet of paper filled with columns of illegible numbers. 'Go ahead, sue me!' he says with a look like a perverse orgasm. He mops his brow, stuffing a wad of bulging banknotes back into his pocket. 'Agh!' he screams, suddenly terrified. 'Look over there, over there! Look!' He points with a Shakespearean finger towards the dark corridor. 'I saw Her!' he whimpers. 'No, no, Père Ubu, it is only the accountant!' 'Don't contradict me! I am old and tired! She prowls the corridors with that smell of the Tagus and of Portuguese hospitals!' He pours himself a big glass of bourbon. He is a bit calmer now. 'Listen, *mon cher*,' he says smiling like a cat. 'The best I can offer is half your

salary. You will get the rest next week in small denom-
inations . . . just don't tell the others! Now, leave me
alone! Leave me to this irascible melancholy, these
Portuguese shadows!'

So you take the cheque from Père Ubu's chubby fingers.
He is doing you a favour. It goes without saying the
cheque isn't drawn on the same bank as last month. Ubu
Publishing is constantly going bankrupt only to rise
again inexplicably. Père Ubu, Ubu with his doe eyes, is
always turning up unlikely banks: Crédit de Lozère,
Bank of Burundi, Banco Vasco da Gama, Banco de
Panico, etc.

When Ubu, the Erl-king, the overweight goblin, first
hired the uncle, he did so more or less in these words:
'My child, my child, I'm thinking of creating a new
imprint, an affiliate of Ubu Publications. What would
you say, my dear, to being LITERARY DIRECTOR of
Megalo Publishing? You shall have gold and women
and sizable rations of rum!'

The uncle found himself sitting behind a partition at
a desk in a corridor. For three years. Trampled under-
foot by the fury of Ubu.

The uncle's responsibilities are extraordinary: drinking
at book launches, plundering the book vault, leaving
horrendous manuscripts to rot, rejecting manuscripts
Ubu published a week earlier, writing vague back-cover
blurbs, answering the phone, etc.

At Ubu, the telephone rings and rings. No one wants
to answer it, to be shouted at by suppliers, irritable

authors, translators, Père Ubu, etc. 'Père Ubu,' you warble into the phone, 'I've got some guy on line . . .' 'Leave me the fuck alone!' he roars and hangs up.

Then there are the manuscripts.

'Yes, madam, I'm in charge of unsolicited manuscripts . . . *The Exceptional Goldfish*? . . . The title does sound familiar now that you mention it . . . Seven hundred pages, yes I remember! . . . It is out with a reader, madam . . . Exactly . . . I'm sorry? *Bubule*? *Bubule* died in terrible agony? Oh, I see, Bubule was the name of your goldfish . . . I understand . . . So you suggest I read the last hundred pages . . . the death scene . . . Okay . . . Oh, really? . . . Scale by scale? Uh-huh . . . Oh, my God! . . . Of course . . . I understand . . . Wouldn't even eat his water fleas at the end . . . Yes . . . I see . . . yes . . . So *Bubule* had children? . . . A sequel? . . . You're writing a sequel . . . nine hundred pages . . . three children . . . Of course . . . The print run? I'm afraid *Bubule* is currently being scrutinized by the editorial committee composed of me, myself, madam, and I . . . I'm sorry? . . . About two years, madam . . . Yes, I'm afraid we do receive a lot of manuscripts . . . Of course . . . I look forward to volume two . . .'

Then there are the bookshops:

'I'm sorry, what did you say the title was? . . .*Tilly and Odd Go to Sea*? . . . And your customer says it is published by Ubu-Import-Export? . . . No . . . Doesn't ring any bells . . . It's not one of ours . . .

Tilly and Odd Go to Sea . . . *Tilly and Odd Go to Sea* . . . Just a minute . . . Just a minute . . . You're sure that's the title? A new translation that we published recently? Maybe you're thinking of *The Iliad* and *The Odyssey* . . .'

The Ubu Publishing booth for the Salon du Livre is pitch black. Only the multicoloured skeletons are missing. 'They're too fragile!' Mère Ubu explains. The company pennant flutters from a mast. Père Ubu's ensign is visible from afar, striking terror into every heart. Nearby ships are chary. Ubu the behemoth dons his three-cornered hat and embarks upon the book fair at the Grand Palais for a week of madness and hard drinking. Once they've stowed six or seven tonnes of provisions under the watchful, angry gaze of the medusa, the sailors flop onto the ebony chairs. It is five o'clock. 'Mère Ubu! Slattern! Damnable carcass! Where the devil is my bourbon?' 'In the stockroom, where it always is, my dear,' she replies, flattered. 'Five cases of it. And there is ice tinkling in the ice chest, my love,' she murmurs. 'Then weigh the anchor, it is time for us to ship out!' Unfortunately at that moment officials are circling in their little tugboats. They're waving white handkerchiefs. The Minister of Culture would like to visit this remarkable stand. It is Jack LeShark. 'I'll have nothing to do with that cesspit, that sewer rat! This is my ship!' yells Ubu. 'Let not the wolf's malodorous feet set foot upon the soil of this Ubuesque land!' But Jack, with his shark's-tooth smile, is insistent. The vast jellyfish that is Mère Ubu, menacing and obsequious, sways in front of him. She brushes off his compliments with a disgusted smirk. Vivaldi's *Gloria* bursts from the loudspeakers of the Grand Palais. The party has begun.

The Salon du Livre is the ultimate trip, one long, sleepless night, exhausting and delicious. You drink. You pillage. You rape. Life is fleeting. Life is fawning. Here you are aboard the most sublime ship of fools. Meanwhile, from all around, from the tragic, fruited grottos, along the forgotten byways, comes the rustle of books, the inexhaustible motherlode, piled high with glory and despair. 'Ah,' says Ubu. 'Listen! Mère Ubu, you old harridan, Listen to them sing and sob! Before we go to our graves, united and jobless like the damnable Portuguese, the mason petrified within the brick, the banker in a lava flow of anxiety, toe to toe, dentures to vagina, listen to them . . . just listen . . .' He pours himself a vast swig of the liquor of Polyphemus. 'Oh Mère Ubu! Can it be true that all men must die? Far from these beakers full of the warm South, far from the tumult, the glorious chaos! By the Gods of Portugal and the Bank of Swindle, can it be true?' 'Père Ubu, Erl-king, calm down! You have published books! Can't you hear them singing all around you!' 'Oh Mère Ubu! Shall we meet again in Paradise? Will you be perched on the stool of purity? Will we be seated at the right hand of Saint Jérôme? . . . and what of the Place Saint-Sulpice? Will there be a place for Saint-Sulpice? Garden sheds in the

June sunshine!! Bearded halfwits!! Garrulous podiums in the jumbled shadows!!'

As five o'clock approaches, everyone at the Ubu booth starts to look at his or her watch eagerly. And at every other booth. 'It is time!' declare the employees. They go down to the stockroom to fetch up the Yankee bourbon. Sharks start to circle: authors, failures, pretentious wankers, all the glorious castaways of the House of Ubu arrive, drawn by the light glinting from the whisky glasses like ships to small coastal lighthouses. 'Brothers!' sings the innkeeper with lips of malt. 'how happy I am to see you. Don't be surprised that there isn't a single copy of your books on these tables! The vermin have been shirking!' Ubu turns towards his galley slaves: 'Miserable scum! Lay these eminent gentlemen's books upon these black tables with due care and no hypocrisy! And let them have your ill-deserved chairs.' He is sweating. He straddles two chairs, spilling over like jelly.

'Brothers! Let me tell you the latest exploits of that pathetic character!' A stubby finger points out the flabby uncle. The henchmen and the third-rate writers among Ubu's cortège tremble and chuckle. 'Last night, this degenerate – a man I give one hundred rations a month – this hack I was fool enough to take aboard, was up to his old tricks, and very droll too, 'pon my word!' The uncle smiles and waves. 'Hold your tongue, uncle! I'll tell the story! And stop knocking back my bourbon!' thunders Ubu. 'So, last night

the uncle attended a cocktail party organized by Upstart
Editions . . .' In Ubu's parlance, Upstart Editions refers
to one of the oldest publishing houses in the kingdom.
'There he hobnobbed with big shots that I, thankfully,
cannot afford to publish. The bastards have already
been paid twice over. As usual the uncle was pie-eyed!
He spent the whole evening convinced that Madame
Upstart, that bottle blonde with her pulchritudinous
pussy, was the Minister of Justice! Ha! Ha! Ha! I
admit there is a certain resemblance . . . Anyway, when
the hoi polloi went upstairs to the couple's apartment
to feast and drink themselves senseless, this guileless
prawn was shocked to see the Keeper of the Seals, the
Minister of Justice herself, arranging plates, chairs,
tables . . .' Ubu suddenly adopts a stupid voice:
'"*Madame Minister! I see they have got you playing
the scullery maid tonight!*" says our friend the uncle,
mystified. Now just imagine him, with his effluvial
stench of champagne!' Ubu continues. 'Ha! ha! ha! He
even went so far as to pinch her buttocks. Right in
front of her husband! Ha! ha! ha!' Ubu stops: 'Mère
Ubu! Worthless wretch! Fetch more bourbon for me
and for these crook-backed gentlemen!' He returns to
the uncle's adventures. 'This child even went so far as
to micturate in the ensuite bathroom of the master
bedroom, in the process disturbing some heiress
slumped in front of a television watching reruns! Ha!
ha! ha! He happened upon Madame Upstart's black
lingerie, which he purloined for me! Everyone at the

Salon has been hunting high and low for this brassiere, but I have it!' From his money pocket he takes the stolen garment. 'Gentlemen! We shall hoist the spoils of war upon the mast of Ubu Publishing and goad the flagship of French publishing!'

For the employees of Ubu Publishing the Salon du Livre is exhausting. There are the days. And then again there are the nights. During 'holy week' Ubu's largesse is unbounded. He is very nearly generous. He finances late-night banquets. Between the night of the banquet and the arrival of the bailiffs there is a gap of about two months. The restaurant where these banquets take place changes regularly.

Staggering slightly, everybody splits up, piling into a truck and a bunch of cars: established authors, blue-eyed newcomers, ready to pierce the night, shrouded in alcohol and the brevity of life. 'Let us go!' says Ubu, Ubu the magnificent, the execrable. 'Let us go in search of winking shellfish! Come hither, Mère Ubu!' Whole tanks of lobster are set aside in readiness for Their Highnesses, and one pictures Ubu howling somewhere in his black car: 'Mère Ubu! Lazybones! You've gone to the wrong street! Meanwhile, those bastards are eating all the money I don't have!' And he's right: Ubu Publishing's good-humoured accountant, a bookkeeping brigadier in charge of shady business and precarious book-balancing, is knocking back one whisky after another: 'It doesn't matter! The whole world's insolvent! The whole thing's just a game! So set 'em up, black-and-white barkeep, fatal penguin, pour us some shell oil *while the big bad wolf isn't here!*'

It is in just such a nocturnal setting that the uncle met Bruno Michel, a young, balding man who had already published two books: *To Betray* and *The Pursuit of Glory*. Given that he'd been drinking, Bruno was somewhat appalled by the drunken human detritus everywhere. In fact, a few years later at a New Year's Eve party, at around six in the morning, Bruno will deliver one of his most inspirational epigrams: 'I despise you! I despise you!' he will scream at the other revellers, confused and sweating, like a man waking up during surgery, pointlessly called back to life to suffer more pain, more scratches, without his mummy.

That evening, the uncle and the bald guy hit it off. They remained friends for a number of years. But when you have a career, you don't lumber yourself with friends. Strangely, Bruno himself used to make this very point: he always said that in the end friends betray you. The uncle used to go round and eat frozen food in Bruno's bleak, two-room apartment. They'd stare into the fridge where a pre-packaged something was loitering, they'd discuss it as if it were the flowering of *the minimalist period*. Bruno insisted on forcing the uncle to watch the Sunday night erotic movie and the most moronic programmes on television. Bruno had always wanted a poodle. In fact, Bruno was pretty dog-like himself: sometimes he'd lick the uncle's cheeks and laugh. He'd read Lamartine's *Le Lac* in a wary voice and weep. His mother had abandoned him at birth. 'I want glory and recognition,' he used to say – without a hint of shame or hesitation. He wanted to be a rock star, surrounded by women, but given his scrawny physique and his intelligence, he had become a writer.

They spent all day on the phone together avoiding endless work. Like the uncle, Bruno was appallingly bored. They both felt hunted, as if society were a jungle and they were constantly being forced to find somewhere new to hide, just before their indolence was noticed. The only true profession was writing. A profession that Bruno was beginning to exercise. With great success. As his fame grew, by some curious corollary, his friendship with the uncle waned.

After a while, the uncle got bored working at Ubu Publishing. Economic conditions were inauspicious. A couple of years earlier, Ubu had hired him grandiloquently. Now, he made the uncle the kind of offer only he knew how to make. 'Come in, dear child!' he said in a sugared, plaintive voice. 'Our finances are temporarily catastrophic. Besides, in my immeasurable kindness, a virtue unequalled except perhaps by my sublime sincerity, I've been giving your future some thought. So, what I'd like to do is offer you a *phony real* redundancy or, if you prefer, a *real phony* redundancy!' Having poured a mammoth glassful for the uncle and one for himself, he went on with eyes like manholes. 'Let me explain . . .'

Having listened to Ubu's verbal gymnastics, in which he proposed to make the uncle *provisionally* redundant only to joyously rehire him three months later, the uncle looked at him fondly. 'If I understand you correctly, Ubu my dear, if I accept the *phony real* redundancy I leave without a penny?' 'Precisely! Precisely! And in the case of the *real phony* redundancy, there is no compensation!' He was clearly moved that the uncle had immediately understood the subtlety of this brilliant, munificent stratagem. The uncle was indeed impressed, but opted for *genuine real* redundancy. He had just turned Christ's age.

XIV

Unemployment has a number of distinct advantages: finally, at the age of thirty-five, you can go home and live with your parents. There is only one condition: you have to be single. If you're married, don't worry, unemployment usually leads to a swift divorce.

Thanks to social security, you manage to resist this foetal temptation for two years.

As you were registering at the employment agency, you realized you had it easy: sitting next to you was a fifty-year-old man with a little moustache. He was exceptionally polite. He presented the required papers with great dignity; he had his whole working life meticulously organized in a folder. He was an engineer who had obviously managed to pull himself up by the bootstraps to become a self-effacing middle manager. He was cut down in the middle of this professional trajectory. He was resentful but his resentment was impeccable: the only thing that betrayed his anger was his exaggerated politeness. He was on the road to a nervous breakdown.

You spend your time vaguely preparing for some

arcane interview, half-heartedly looking for a job. The very thought of work makes you throw up. You register with the alumni association of a very fashionable school. This is the mid nineties, even the people you meet here have not been spared unemployment. But they keep trying. All of them have obviously followed a more traditional career path than your own. Your adviser is overworked. She is dumbfounded by your casual manner and is deeply pessimistic.

You have a long list of things that make you want to throw up. With masochistic pleasure you watch the news. The leader of the French Business Confederation has a red cashmere sweater draped round his shoulders. It is summer. He's tanned. He looks as though he's been working out. He's angry that the minimum wage has just been unjustifiably increased. Standing behind him is a bunch of other little shits from his organization. They're all wearing red sweaters over their shoulders. They're attending their summer conference. The mere sight of yogurt-makers and dishwashing-liquid salesmen gathered for a conference seems incongruous to you. What is a CEO? A CEO is someone who would like you to work twelve hours a day for the price of six. He criticizes the State and the government while going cap in hand to them for subsidies. His bidet factory exists only to fund the lavish lifestyle of his family of morons. All of his children have their own cars, fail their baccalaureate three times, spend long periods in the United States, and look down their noses at you.

What is democracy? It is one more on the list of things that make you throw up. In a democratic country, the head of state tells his fellow citizens how much he earns and how much tax he pays. It is a commendable gesture. Among the many possible definitions, a modern democracy is a political system in which prodigiously educated, profoundly lucid and perfectly disinterested citizens elect a representative who will earn more in a year than most of them will see in a lifetime. Besides which, he's usually exposed as a crook and jumps bail.

With considerable dignity, you move into ever-smaller studio apartments. At night, you drown your sorrows in faintly seedy nightclubs. On days when you have an interview lined up, you forget to set your alarm clock or you serenely fail the interview. Now, your social security has run out. Several times already your mother has offered you shelter. In fact, she never really understood why you left the family home at the age of twenty-six. Though she had been prepared to accept you getting a job at the age of twenty-four. You're a man and men are supposed to work. In fact, only men should be allowed to work.

Your mother has never studied or worked a day in her life. This complete lack of education means that she has an unerring ability to put things in a nutshell. She has a sweeping vision of society. She offers opinions on working women, psychoanalysis, the Israeli–Palestinian conflict, etc. Society has been going downhill ever since women went out to work. A career woman buys frozen foods, neglects her children, gets divorced. She is a show-off with a brain. She has orgasms. The aim of psychoanalysis is to create conflict within perfect families. People would understand the Israeli–Palestinian conflict if they met her Jewish neighbour from upstairs, the one who refuses to accept responsibility for the water damage. Actually, none of your mother's opinions are her own. She borrowed this latest opinion from her eldest son, a closet queer who thinks his neighbour is a slut. You're tempted to give them both a slap in the face: they both know that the woman you love is Jewish. Your brother has dinner with his parents nearly every night. He goes to bed at 10:00 p.m. He is rude and overbearing. He loathes women. Actually, he loathes everyone. He adores Proust and probably secretly reads *Hello!* magazine. Even though Proust is pretty Jewish. On the other hand, he was male, *bourgeois* and a closet queer.

You left the family home for the first time at the age of twenty-six. You were hopelessly in love with a girl of twenty. It is thanks to her that you manage to escape the monstrous island where you were almost turned into a swine. It is one of the greatest moments of your life. Your mother is united with you in your joy. A fact she proves four months later when you tell her the girl has left you. Her words are consoling: 'I'm so happy, darling! That girl would never have amounted to anything!' Fortunately, you had friends whose shoulders you could cry on. It doesn't matter: however badly you were hurt, you took a decisive step.

But here you are, back in the very same bedroom
you slept in as a child. The world travellers who have
taken you are still renting the same place after fifty
years. Half a century pacing up and down the same
apartment is definitely at least the equivalent of circum-
navigating the globe. One of their sons lives in the same
building, three floors down. His apartment is a mirror
image of theirs. He lives there with his family. He will
probably have himself buried in the cellar. Another son
lives about five hundred metres away. It takes somewhere between thirty seconds and five minutes for the
mother to get to one of her colonies. Even the fastest
American stealth bomber takes several hours to go and
spy on some distant corner of the planet. Within her
sphere of influence, the mother is more powerful than
the President of the United States. The wallpaper in
your bedroom is the same as ever. You picked it out
yourself when you were twelve years old. You have
also been assigned the room next door – your brother's
old bedroom. It has a pair of twin beds. With your
cat, you settle into this charming two-room apartment
inside the walls of your parents' house. Every time the
cat spots your mother, it gets nervous.

The first few days are strange. Unsurprisingly, you
feel childishly happy. The only thing missing is the
Christmas tree. Your mother explains the rules of the
house: dinner is served at seven-thirty, you must never
leave the freezer door open, the salt and pepper are
kept in the right-hand cupboard, you may store your

beer on the bottom shelf of the fridge. The mammal opens the fridge and shows you her accomplishments. There is a dizzying array of foodstuffs, each methodically labelled with the name of the product and date of purchase. It is a very professional job. The mammal is happy and nervous.

In the weeks before you moved in, you were a nocturnal animal. For a while, you stick to this rhythm and routine. On the third night, you bring home some girl you vaguely know, a regular from the Moloko. Jamila is twenty. She goes clubbing every night. She lives in the suburbs with her aunt. She suffers from angina. At five in the morning, you offer her a bed for the night. She would obviously prefer you to drive her back to the suburbs but you haven't got a car any more. All night, you stroke her breasts distractedly. She moans sleepily. It doesn't go any further. But what difference does it make whether you sleep with her or just watch her? In either case you will have had the illusion of knowing her. Besides, alcohol has already afforded you every worldly pleasure. You're thirty-five, you have several diplomas, a solid past and a middle-class family; Jamila has nothing. But, like you, she is a survivor. For her, failure is a social reality she can never overcome, one she will probably drag with her all her life. For you, it is a temporary, luxurious vacuum.

One night you met a gypsy girl at the Bataclan, a soul in torment like yourself. Basically, she survived by robbing parking meters. Her pockets were stuffed with coins. She had her period that night. She was as drunk as you were. You kissed at dawn on a deserted boulevard, a wounded kiss with no possible future. Then together you went off to endless shots of bourbon. As you were telling her your life story, she said, 'The middle classes are the most liberated people in the world when they go off the rails.' It is probably true. The middle classes have the funds and the knowledge and they have always got a safety net. Rumour has it that you are a lot like some of your father's infamous uncles: sailors and swashbucklers, marriers of prostitutes. Your father could have been like them or he might have been a lesser urban buccaneer like you, hemmed in by his middle-class principles. Not a first-class reprobate but a drunk gifted with curiosity and broad-mindedness. Unfortunately, most men have only two balls: one for their mother, one for their wife, none for themselves.

It is noon. Jamila is snoring. It is Sunday, day of the imperishable Sunday lunch in sophisticated families. You have the sickening feeling of being in a restaurant. The lingering smells of roast meat, the clicking of cutlery, the tinkling of glasses are carried on the breeze to your room. In the distance, the mammal is feverishly working. Lunch is at one o'clock. You make a futile attempt to wake Jamila. You're terrified that your mother will knock on your door at any moment. You have to face the music. Meet her head on in her place of work. The rings of the gas stove are jubilant. The mammal opens the oven, checks the double boiler, rattles the pots. The courses steadily multiply: the inevitable chicken, the salad, the cheeses, the fear of failure. You feel like throwing up. You knocked back your last whisky and Coke at 5 a.m. Still, you sneakily feign an interest in the mammal's creations, enthusiastically sniff the dishes, solicit advice and recipes. You pat her cheek. Scratch her behind the ears. All mammals love to be scratched behind the ears. You feel a certain affection. After all, once upon a time you swam inside her, drank from her placenta. She was your first bar. Then, one day, she reluctantly pushed you out. Now, you drift from bar to bar seeking your measure of primordial liquor. Bars are vast wombs, dim and bustling. The mammal is flattered but she senses something is wrong. You launch into some unbelievable story. Jamila, the body sprawled in your two-room apartment, is definitely not your girl-friend. There has been a misunderstanding. Actually, Jamila is a friend of Toto's. 'Oh yes, one of Toto's young Algerian friends,' you say with a vague smile, still scratching the mammal behind the ears. The mammal is very fond of Toto, *that charming boy Toto*. Actually he's a docile failure who went back to live with his parents leaving six months' unpaid rent. He is completely unthreatening. A man of forty who lives with his parents and hasn't done a day's work in ten years is clearly an ideal sort of friend. The mammal would love to meet Toto's mother, this kindred spirit who has so success-fully emasculated her son. So anyway, last night at about 3 a.m., poor Toto wasn't feeling well, so he went

home. He entrusted Jamila to you. You weren't very
happy about the idea, but since she lived out in Sarcelles
etc. You won't be able join them for Sunday lunch.
Sadly. Your mother is starting to panic. Let us take a
look at a cat in the throes of some inner turmoil. Cats
are of the genus *Felidae*, affectionate mammals endowed
with fur. A cat's brain is comparatively undeveloped.
Stroke it for a while, then push it away roughly. Its tail
twitches in all directions, its ears prick up, it stares
stupidly at you: it struggles with this inexplicable conundrum. A conundrum not unlike the one the little mammal
who gave birth to you is struggling with as she bustles
around the kitchen. On the one hand, she is delighted
you're so considerate and that you're still friends with
that charming boy Toto. On the other hand, somewhere
in the two-room apartment next door lies some sort of
prostitute whose very presence is a danger to the Sunday
family lunch.

At about one o'clock, Jamila wakes up and effort-
lessly takes over the bathroom. You have already promised you will disinfect the bathroom after her
insalubrious wallowings. Your mother has already
whisked off the contaminated sheets. Jamila is unaware
of being deep in enemy territory: in the distance, a herd
of mammals is devouring a free-range chicken. You can
hear raised voices from the dining room. Your elder
brother is obviously livid. His parents are letting this
freeloader who's only been in the house a few days do
whatever he likes. He doesn't get up until noon! He

fornicates with immigrant whores! He has a point: at
that very moment you are sodomizing Jamila in the
bathroom. The wash basin she is hanging onto vibrates
precariously. She moans. Sadly, your mother is on her
way back to the kitchen carrying the remains of this
year's fifty-second chicken. She asks if everything is all
right. 'I'm just cleaning Jamila!' you explain. You meant
to say 'the wash basin' obviously. 'It's okay, I'll take
care of it!' replies your mother. 'Fuck off. Mind your
own business!' shouts the beautiful Jamila. Fortunately
you managed to drown her out by insisting that you
will clean the wash basin yourself with Mister Clean.
'There is no need to shout,' the mammal remarks as
the elegant Jamila howls: 'Fuck off! Can't you tell he's
fucking me up the ass?' At about three o'clock, you
discreetly spirit Jamila away without introducing her
to *that bitch who was seriously getting on my tits*.

After this incident, you adopt a more leisurely pace,
though you still avoid Sunday lunch. From time to time
you entertain girls from your world. You are careful
to introduce them simply as friends. Your family affectionately sizes them up: the divorcée who was nice but
terribly dull, the teacher who seemed friendly but wasn't
very bright, etc.

Then the day comes when you have to leave. You
finally got a job. Why this year rather than last year
or the year before? Because you're in touch with the
real world again. For a year now you have been working part time. Making the journey to this extremely

rich, deeply Catholic school, where everyone sleeps with everyone else, means getting up at six in the morning. All the inherent qualities of reality flood back: the cold, the dark, the commute. The school is set in a huge parkland scattered with chapels. You go to mass regularly and stand beside your students pretending to sing. Figures of monks glide through the polished hallways. You overhear wonderful snatches of conversation: 'Obviously, there is no such thing as Christian mathematics . . . but there is a Christian approach to teaching mathematics!' You're surprised by the number of blonde females among the first-year teachers. They all have blue eyes and big breasts. This is because the first-year department is managed by a kindly, married, Christian womaniser. Most of the blondes live in Saint-Cloud or Neuilly. They all wear diamond wedding rings. You salute their extraordinary courage which is tantamount to charity. You have never done any teaching but your CV and your impeccable family won them over. Now here you are teaching Latin. Even though you quite clearly mentioned that you hadn't done Latin for twenty years. It doesn't matter, they're only beginners, you can con them. Besides, you're hardly the only incompetent: most of your pretty colleagues are just as bad. The most important thing is to teach *in a Christian manner.* With this in mind, you take certain liberties with your subject. The manual insists on putting accents over the words. Never mind! In a gesture worthy of Pinel, the celebrated lunatic liberator, you cross out all the accents and celebrate this emancipation with a clever remark: 'Accents are always wrong!' you declare in front of thirty young Christians. You carefully choose texts and exercises well within your abilities. Whenever you encounter an unexpected problem, you encourage your students to play up. In fact, over the course of the year, you shrewdly allow the class to become a generalized bedlam, thereby slowing your progress in the increasingly tricky curriculum. Within six months, you're a past master in the art of spinning out a five-line translation *ad nauseam* over a pleasing pandemonium.

And so, at the age of thirty-seven, the little mammal leaves its parents once again. Your mother has got used to having you around. She is not going to let you go without a fight. Your father won't offer you much help in leaving the warren. He's relieved that you have a job, obviously, but he will not have his wife contradicted. You will have a battle on your hands.

You finally leave ten kilos heavier, with a permanent aftertaste of cold chicken, memories of unemployment, and the feeling that you're missing out on the important things in life. Anger begins to well in your brain. Your slave blood hums softly.

XV

As we've seen, a job is an occupation that can ruin half your life, possibly more. The uncle spent a long time drifting from job to job before finding one that didn't give him this appalling feeling.

What is a teacher? Let us take a look at this simple diagram:

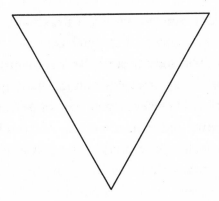

The first time he saw it, the uncle shouted 'Vagina!' It happened during a training day charmingly entitled 'The Teacher: A Mediator in Knowledge Acquisition'. The uncle was slumped at the back of the classroom, an aging wreck only just saved from unemployment, surrounded by eager young colleagues. The trainer was savouring the effect of his diagram, keeping everyone in spellbinding suspense. That's when the uncle shouted 'Vagina!' Any sensible soul would have reacted with the same grace, the same quick-witted intelligence. The teaching community seems mostly to be made up of women who read at least one book every year, usually something that won a literary prize, a controversial book full of sex or the latest issue of *House & Garden*. This annual read enhances a cultural infrastructure that consists of *Belle du Seigneur*, some books by Daniel Pennac or Le Clézio (whose poster hangs above their beds), and a handful of the classics that they reread every year with renewed audacity, usually plays. They're obsessed with the theatre. These arty women usually run workshops at the school, something that confers on them a sort of municipal, and in a manner of speaking political, notoriety. They have a mission. Every year in some magnificently multiracial suburb, in the *Jacques Brel Arena*, they stage a play pitched somewhere between Racine and Mamadou Gnou. Who is Mamadou Gnou? No one knows. The play is usually called *Colours of the World, My Black Neighbour, Islam, Mon Amour*, and, more rarely, *The Vagina Diatribes*. They are highly praised for this work, which is the only thing standing between the suburbs and ethnic violence. Usually, they are morons. They are divorced and dead inside. But because they're teachers this is more difficult to spot than it might be in the rest of the population.

The whole national education system was nothing more than one big vagina. The uncle's comment was completely justifiable. But the trainer, a gentle, bearded man, flinched. He gave a knowing smile, thinking they were playing up to him, a ruse he was all too familiar with. He was a teacher at an exemplary secondary school that had pupils from at least thirty different ethnic backgrounds. They brawled amicably in a schoolyard adorned with naive frescos. He had bags under his eyes. His off-site training, his sick leave and his psychiatric outpatient appointments were a welcome breath of fresh air in an otherwise fulfilling life. He reasoned with the uncle. He talked about the 'pedagogic triangle' with genuine, audacious intellectual passion. Let us study the pedagogic triangle for a moment:

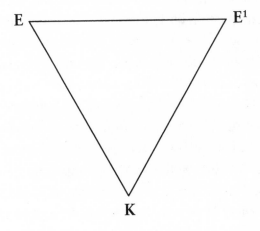

The education sciences, as we can see, are particularly subtle and enlightening. It is not for nothing that the educators who formulated them consider them to be sciences. The uncle scratched his head. He wasn't the only one. Some of his colleagues scratched their armpits and grunted. With a commanding gesture, the bearded one, the French teacher with his multidisciplinary background, joyfully wrote out these dazzling formulae: 'E = Educator', 'E^1 = Educatee', 'K = Knowledge'. The uncle, who was beginning to understand the problem, launched into a brilliant commentary. 'If I understand you correctly,' he said, 'each of the parties in the system is equal. E is not superior to E^1 vis à vis K . . .' The bearded man stared at him, his eyes shining with gratitude. 'Yes! That's right! That's absolutely right!' The uncle was a past master in the art of prostitution. He went on, ingenuously, enthusiastically: 'It is not a matter of passing on knowledge. The Educator knows no more than the Educatee.' The bearded man was falling in love with the uncle. 'Furthermore,' ventured the uncle, who was feeling particularly inspired that day, 'it might even be preferable if the Educator knows less than the Educatee, if I may put forward the paradox . . .' The bearded man gave a joyous yelp. Here, in the person of the uncle, he had a disciple. 'Yes! Yes! That's it! Oh, yes!' The uncle deftly soft-soaped the instructor: 'Of course, that would be a paradox . . . We wouldn't go so far . . . rather, let us say that E must guide E^1 in the attainment of K . . .' The

bearded man let out a series of little moans: 'Oh yes!
Yesssss! The Educatee becomes an agent of his own
education!' Excited now, the uncle expounded his
visionary argument. In the end, he proved that E and
K were obsolete and would soon disappear to the
benefit of E^1. He grabbed the bearded man's tumes-
cent felt-tip and brilliantly sketched what was to
become the 'pedagogic circle':

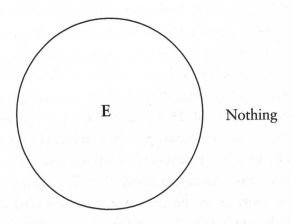

The bearded man noisily started to cum. 'Some people
might say,' the uncle continued, 'that ignorant teachers are making a mockery of education . . . Rebels
might dare to distort the concept of the "pedagogic
circle"':

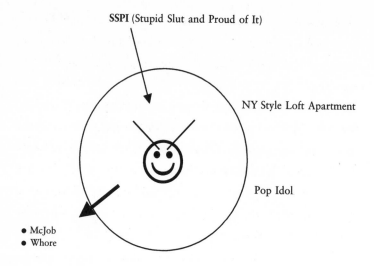

'But these educational fundamentalists will soon be in the minority and will be shipped off to rest homes!' bringing his speech to a close as the instructor, on his knees, sucked his cock and purred.

Some time later, he found out that the bearded man had been stabbed at his school. His colleagues staged a twenty-four-hour wildcat strike. The Educatee apologized to the 'beardy bastard' – his words – and was suspended for a week. This was the start of a period of indefinite sick leave for the instructor. Soon afterwards, the uncle received a letter from him. In it, he thanked the uncle and congratulated him on his contribution to the training day. He briefly recapitulated the principles of the pedagogic triangle for his disciple. Lastly, he told the uncle that he was in the process of writing an article on aggressive behaviour patterns in the scholastic milieu. 'Buy the September issue of the *Oise Valley Educational Supplement*!' he exulted.

This is how the uncle quickly became a practised whore. He hung out with educationalists from the teachers' colleges, most of them losers, geeks or both. He learned the jargon: heterogeneity, remediation, ability grouping, pre-acquired skills, etc. What is a 'pre-acquired skill'? Let us examine the following hypothesis: you would like your final-year students to be able to draw a red line using a ruler. This is your *goal*. You're aware that it is an ambitious task. But you're determined to succeed: you're eager, methodical and, most important, you have learned how to formulate exceptional 'teaching modules'. In week one of your teaching module – there are six weeks in all – you assure yourself that your pupil has mastered two 'pre-acquired skills' vital to the attainment of his goal: the ability to distinguish between a ruler and a pen and the ability to distinguish between a red pen and a blue pen. In an ideal world, if your colleagues who teach first grade have done their job properly, this shouldn't be a problem. Even so, you set aside week two of your module for 'remediation': given the 'heterogeneity' of pupils, there will always be seven or eight who master the first skill but not the second or the second but not the first or neither. Remediation, therefore, is essential. Now we come to the nitty-gritty: week three is dedicated to the simul-taneous manoeuvring of ruler and pen, but there is no drawing of lines. To introduce this Herculean task into your 'pedagogic progression' too early would fuck up the whole module: even the least simple-minded, least spineless, least corrupt inspector would record such a basic error in your homework notebook and might hinder repayments on your, admittedly pitiful, house. In week four, you will begin to focus on draw-ing a line. You might productively use 'co-operative learning'. Co-operative learning involves dividing the class in groups. It is chaos. Educatees love co-operative learning. At the end of week four you make an 'ongoing assessment', something not to be confused with the 'final appraisal' scheduled for the end of the module. You are not unduly harsh in this assessment: crude lines, even if drawn freehand, even in blue pen, will suffice. Higher marks are given for lines drawn in red pen without a ruler or those traced using a ruler but with a pen of a different colour. Full marks are awarded when both directives have been respected. Over the course of the year, you will organize regu-lar 'skills reinvestment' sessions. For example, a module entitled 'Underlining an Essay Title' lasting no more than seven weeks will rely heavily on these pre-acquired skills.

The uncle spent a marvellous year in this area lapped by the waters of the Oise. He was in love. Every morn-ing, the train swept past the network of canals and market gardens. He was learning vital life-lessons and laughing a great deal. It was like a summer camp: counsellors offered workshops on yoga, African dance, theatre.

A second training day, enthusiastically organized by a principal and a school counsellor, forced him to seriously rethink. What is a school counsellor? Nowadays he – or more usually she – eagerly reads books entitled *Teenagers at Risk, Anorexia and Academic Failure, Little Brown Bear,* etc. Psychology is her only passion. She likes nothing better than a fresh divorce. She detects hidden meanings in pallid complexions and bags under the eyes. She is always the first with news of a suicide attempt – sadly botched, since one less file would be progress. She spends staff meetings endlessly rationalizing academic failure. As indeed you do, though more succinctly and not quite in the same terms. But there is no point trying to tell her that some students are just terminally stupid, that some people are just born lazy. You will wind up with a reputation as a troublemaker: God has not endowed all His children with similar talents. The principal handed out some folded slips of paper. They had obviously been scribbled out over lunch, since they're covered with grease and red wine stains. As is the principal's green polo shirt. The uncle was lucky, he picked the right piece of paper: 'You're walking down the hall. As you pass a group of students, you hear: "Hey, fucker!" How do you

react?' The uncle ad libbed a daring response: 'I
pretend I didn't hear anything. I walk on with dignity.
I ignore the hail of spitballs etc.' The two pathetic
idiots concur: this as a rational response. Let us note
that the uncle did encounter a very similar situation
shortly afterwards when a student he didn't recognize presented him with a hand from which rose a
lone, erect middle digit; the uncle told the kid to go
fuck himself. The pupil was shocked . . . But, let us
get back to the slips of paper. One of the uncle's
friends wasn't as lucky: 'You are leaving the school
grounds. Outside the gates stands an angry father
waiting for you with a pump-action shotgun. How
do you react?' Now, *there* was a question. No one
could think of an answer. The principal belched and
looked confidently at Madame Groin. With due
solemnity, the school counsellor explained. In fact,
you simply needed to turn the problem on its head
. . . Most aggressive behaviour is just a mask to hide
a person's pain . . . Most bullies are victims . . .
Obviously this father was in terrible pain . . . You
simply needed to show him that you meant no harm
. . . That you weren't going to savagely attack him
. . . 'You see,' she said in a maternal tone, 'all you
need to do is smile, just smile, and gently, mysteri-
ously stroke the gleaming barrel of his shotgun . . .'
The principal interrupted Madame Groin: 'Of course,
cases like this are extremely rare . . .' Though there
had been the case of the mother with the axe last

summer. Someone had managed to catch her with a lasso. No easy task, since she was hiding in a tree at the time. 'Remember that, Madame Groin?' said the principal, making a gesture as if lassoing.

XVI

The Oise Valley is famous for the enormity of its academic failure, which is among the worst in France. To mention some of the charming towns of the Oise Valley: Garges-lès-Gonesse, Gonesse, Goussainville, Sarcelles, Stains, Villiers-le-Bel, etc. As he's just starting out, the uncle is required to teach in two separate towns in the region. This is a privilege reserved for novices, who have an exceptionally hectic timetable. The bus from Waterloo Secondary School to Walt Disney College takes a mere half hour. The passengers all wear djellabas.

Walt Disney College is a campus in the classical style consisting of three large buildings, a scattering of charming prefabs and a beautiful park. There is a car park that serves as an escape route for the teachers. No one can work out how violence became endemic among these leafy trees and frolicsome birds. If anything deserves to survive the ravages of our species, surely it is trees and birds. Then again, birds are evil bastards; they slaughter one another under the cover of foliage and savagely devour raw insects. Besides, they wake up at four in the morning and make a deafening racket. You never really feel safe around birds.

The headmaster of Walt Disney College is a pig. He's vulgar, spineless and incompetent and has surrounded himself with group of young teachers in his own image: charming individuals who have all found a niche in this fiasco. They play cards and go drinking together after class. At home, they watch reruns or play on their PlayStations. They are suspicious of anything new. Cowardice, mediocrity, cynicism, popularity-seeking, insincerity and fraud are the most common traits of the Walt Disney staff.

Then there are the cripples. Some of the cripples are close to retirement, others are pushing fifty, still others are barely thirty. They have bought houses close to the school where they are slowly dying. The journey from this world to the next will barely change them at all. Their mental activity is already almost nonexistent. They spend most of their time talking about how they fixed the boiler last weekend. They nervously ask about the secondary school syllabus. Their worst fear is to wind up teaching in a secondary school. Already they have fallen behind their own pupils in the subject they're teaching. They have stopped reacting. They have come to expect the worst. For some, stress and humiliation have become like a drug.

In the end, everyone becomes accustomed to hell. Once you become accustomed to it, the real distinction is between those who accept it and those will never accept it. A normal person could not spend longer than a year at Walt Disney College.

You know the score from the very first day. Scientists are busy scouring the universe for alien life forms. They're looking in the wrong place: the aliens have already landed at Walt Disney College and at colleges like it the world over. A fine day begins, a bout consisting of eight rounds, a bell marking the end of each round. The first fights break out. The teachers wear jaded, blasé smiles. Pupils playfully jostle and insult them. This is an absolutely normal form of communication. The new kids in first year look a bit nervous. Every day, the fire brigade and the police are called. Teachers lock themselves in classrooms. Gangs run riot in the halls screaming and kicking doors. Projectiles fired from the scenic park sometimes come through the windows. Everything goes back to normal. It is the first week of term.

The first week of term and the last week before the summer break are the highlights of the year at Walt Disney College. The last week is probably even more interesting than the first. Newbies are advised to leave the school in groups because of the projectiles. A lone teacher makes a tempting target. A valiant brigade rushing for the exit is more daunting, more likely to dissuade. Despite all this, academic appraisal at Walt Disney is very lenient: every student graduates to the next year. There is no question of forcing a fourteen-year-old who has daringly scaled the dizzying heights of second year to stay in school any longer. So no one really knows why the last week is even more fun than the others, why gangs of pupils want to storm the staff room. It is baffling.

The supervisors at Walt Disney College spend their time playing cards in a small room. It is almost impossible to distinguish them from the pupils, especially the tall black guys. These are the 'youth workers'. They're not really unemployed just yet. They're either students or dealers. No one really knows which. They don't care about the general chaos. They think the whole system is shit. They're right.

The headmaster loves to write. It is one of his favourite activities, along with eating, shouting, being insulted, having chairs thrown through his windows, etc. He bombards new teachers with first-rate teaching advice. He reminds them of the basics of teaching, which boils down to not making waves. If someone spits at you, for example or you have your wallet stolen, which, let's face it, are minor and completely acceptable offences, there is no point reporting it and demanding that action be taken. 'Let me make this crystal clear, cherished colleagues: the school administration will not support you. It is your job to earn respect!'

The school counsellor has bags under her eyes. She puts the headmaster's principles into operation with commendable enthusiasm. There is no point relying on her in times of trouble: she sides with the pupils; in fact, she becomes aggressive if you actually report one

of them. Her strategy seems to work quite well for a
few weeks. Then you start to see her wandering the
halls in floods of tears. The uncle takes a certain pleasure in offering her tissues. It is a depressing fact but
teaching forcibly teaches you one of the fundamental
truths of human nature: humanity favours whips over
hugs. And if you must go round on hugging, make sure
you have a whip in the other hand.

The biggest whores are the teachers in the headmaster's clique. Most of them are between twenty-five and
thirty. They're from the 'pedagogic triangle' school. This
pox-ridden triangle churns out popularity-seeking
government ministers, spineless, ruthlessly ambitious
school inspectors, dictatorial educationalists, boorish
teachers, cynics, morons, etc. What are the whores'
teaching methods? Their pupils learn complicated things.
In fourth year, they copy out vocabulary lists or colour
in geometric shapes in neatly kept copybooks. The
whores love copybooks. They warn their pupils: a messy
copybook will be awarded a C. The whores are very
fond of holding debates about football, violence, the
Oise Valley, anything and everything. Oral is important.
The students do very well in their orals. Nothing less
than a B– in their orals. This means that the average
grades in the whores' classes are excellent. A student at
Walt Disney who has been in one of the whores' classes
will graduate into third year with straight As, only to
see his grades nose-dive ten points. The whores claim
this is the famous third-year blip. Besides, a D average

isn't too bad. The students don't understand why their new teachers mark so harshly. The change makes them nervous and bad-mannered. Especially when Mr. Whore tells them that Mr. New-Guy *is* really harsh, but he will only be here for a year. 'Take the case of Fatima,' explains Mr. Whore. Fatima is thirteen and in first year. Okay, she is illiterate, but she keeps her copybook very neat. And she is very lively in her orals. Mr. Whore gives her a C, Mr. Nasty gives her an F. She likes Mr. Whore because he rates her oral skills very highly. It is true she spends all her time talking to her neighbours. Fatima is a social animal. And since she doesn't understand the class, she has to keep busy. Still, the uncle is quite fond of fat Fatima. She has a good heart. She is actively acquiring skills that will be useful in her future profession: she is always willing to pick up rubbish, wipe down the desks or tidy away the chairs at the end of the day.

The administration at Walt Disney is effectively balanced by the presence of a union activist. What is a union activist? He is generally 'out of class'. Actually, he sits on National Education committees awarding promotions and other little perks. He eagerly demonstrates the liberal trade unionist principles of, and his solidarity with, his fellow-teachers – particularly the new recruits – by assigning the best classes and the easiest workload to himself. He's usually a loudmouth and will generally argue with the headmaster on principle while secretly doing under-the-table deals. He knows a couple of local

journalists whom he uses on occasion. It might be said
that he doesn't have to be a union activist to exhibit such
noble principles. This is true: a lot of teachers become
noteworthy in their school and are prepared to play the
dirtiest tricks. The uncle remembers a particularly instruc-
tive year. It was in a lovely secondary school in Clichy.
The principal was anything but a joker. He was a powerful man and compassionate as an iceberg. His school
looked like a brand-new freezer. Induction there was a
very humane process: the eight female academics who
taught French agreed among themselves to palm the
worst classes off on the new teachers; the brilliant math-
ematician who taught the only preparatory class for the
grandes écoles affectionately regarded you as a cock-
roach; other teachers politely asked what the hell you
were doing in this classroom that had been theirs since
time immemorial, etc.

At Walt Disney College, no one really knows why
they need a union activist. The teachers here are
promoted on the basis of their apathy and their absence
of critical judgement. There are no union meetings, no
wildcat strikes, not even minor skirmishes between
smokers and non-smokers. Any educational establish-
ment worthy of the name is usually a pitched battle
between smokers and non-smokers. There are regular
rowdy verbal hostilities. Because tobacco divides people
along fundamental political lines. Even people who
don't usually allow themselves to be caught up in social
strife quickly wake up and become committed activists

when it comes to hounding smokers. At Walt Disney College, however, everything is fine. The union activist is a fifty-year-old blonde who rushes around nervously. She always wears white: white tracksuits, white socks, white shoes. She must have a vast wardrobe. All that white is alarming. You cannot help but wonder. You'd need to do some research. To understand the woman's multifaceted personality, you would have to be able to answer the crucial question: why does she always wear white, and nothing but white? She looks like a menopausal majorette or an alpine hunter. She has something to do with the teachers' college. She teaches English.

Were we to classify teachers according to intellectual abilities – something we would be reluctant to do – and obviously allowing for the numerous exceptions, our much-loved colleagues who teach English would be lumped together with biology, physics and chemistry teachers. Someone who teaches biology – what we now call the *life sciences* and the *earth sciences*, two subtly distinct subjects – makes a living out of buggering frogs with thermometers and then dissecting them. Sometimes he masturbates a cricket with a pair of tweezers. A physics or chemistry teacher rarely puts in an appearance in the staff room: he's busy washing test tubes in his lab or staring at a photo of Max Planck or Einstein with a flicker of hatred in his eyes. And English teachers, well, they speak English. This alone is an impressive phenomenon. The powerful muscles they use in the acquisition of language have to be exercised regularly. Otherwise – well, no one actually knows what would happen.

The Walt Disney College majorette is a slut. One day, the principal pins an article from *France-Soir* in a very prominent position on the staff room notice board. He organizes a drinks party with school canteen pâté. The majorette is tense but triumphant. The principal explains the difference between *France-Soir* and *Le Parisien*. *France-Soir* is a much more prestigious newspaper, given that it has a national circulation. You don't quite catch everything he's saying because his mouth is full of pâté. He smells heavily of sweat. What does the article say? The reporter did considerable journalistic work. You can sense a staunch ethical code. He interviewed the principal and the majorette and therefore gained a broad perspective on Walt Disney College. Apparently the majorette-cum-union-activist speaks on behalf of all of her colleagues. While not denying that there are minor problems due to its background, the journalist states that this former powder keg of a school has become a haven of peace and harmony since the arrival of the new principal. 'One of the most peaceful in the region,' in fact. Quoting an English teacher 'deeply committed to her work,' the journalist explains that the 'fairy tale success of Walt Disney College' is due to the 'innovative' teaching methods, to 'intensive teamwork' and to an 'exceptional empathy' between members of the scholastic community. And so on. The whores tease the principal a little: after an article like this he's surely guaranteed a transfer! For some time now he's been hoping for a job as principal at a school for hotel management. There, in the shade of the Vosges, he will be able to live out his days eating and drinking to his heart's content and once a year having some minor government officials around for drinks. His mouth waters. The local education authority is pleased. As is the Minister.

III

Dirty Linen

XVII

The uncle's sex life is a disaster, though it has to be said, it got off to a bad start.

In the latter half of the twentieth century, some years after the conquest of the moon, kindly school doctors divided the adolescent world in two. You came out of the yearly school physical with one of two obligatory labels: 'pre-pubescent' or 'post-pubescent'. These men had the delicacy not to tattoo the information on your cock; they simply wrote it up in the records that catalogued every beast in the French herd. The uncle, it was decided, was on the dark side. As a result, he started to enhance his underpants with sundry items: ping-pong balls, handkerchiefs, etc. His family, who were also people of extraordinary refinement, made his life much easier by never discussing sex with him. So for years the uncle thought he still had not gone through puberty, something that proved a serious setback in losing his virginity and was a source of agony he now finds comical.

Let us go back a bit. The uncle is three or four years old. He is sitting on a gas stove. The gas stove, like

the horse or the microwave, is one of man's great
triumphs. It became commonplace in the postwar years.
It is used for cooking foodstuffs. It has a metal cover.
And so, we see the uncle on the cover of a gas stove
at some indefinite moment during the bleak 1960s. His
mother has decided to take him for a walk in some
park. He clearly disagrees. He pisses on her while she
is dressing him. For the only time in his life, he uses
his penis with absolute naturalness.

What is a caliper rule? It is a metal device used
for measuring volume and diameter with absolute
precision. If, for example, you wanted to calculate
the size of a walnut, you would use a caliper rule.
For this reason, it is particularly recommended for
measuring your balls. When he was sixteen or seventeen, the uncle knew by heart the average size of the
testicle at the various stages of its development. He
was a specialist in the use of the caliper rule. The
volume of the testicle varies noticeably according to
time of day, temperature, frequency of masturbation,
etc. The two millimetres gained each morning melt
away by afternoon. From the available evidence, the
uncle presumed that he was still not post-pubescent.
The reason for this, obviously, was his frenzied
recourse to onanism, the ravages of which had been
feverishly documented in the eighteenth century by
Samuel-Auguste Tissot, physician, Swiss citizen,
Protestant. The uncle dubbed his infirmity the 'hazelnut syndrome' and suffered in silence, always putting

off till tomorrow the brief visit to the doctor that would have put an end to his heavenly torment.

Should teenagers be forbidden all pornographic material? No, quite the opposite. Pornography is a source of extremely reliable information and may spare them much needless suffering. If you have something you want to hide from your children, do so casually, in plain sight. In the TV guide, carefully circle the starting times of a handful of masterpieces: *Sex Starved Sluts, The Doctor Likes Huge Pricks*, etc. The uncle is sorry that he lived through his adolescence in the 1970s when pornography was scarcer and harder to get hold of than it is today. The first time he saw a porn mag at a friend's house, he realized that he'd made a terrible mistake: not only had nature not neglected him, as a matter of fact it had been particularly generous in the size of one crucial organ. Realising that he was tired of fighting, he eventually made the leap from pre- to post-pubescent in the arms of a young woman he trusted completely. He was twenty years old. And so a man was made.

Your years spent convinced you were suffering from 'hazelnut syndrome' have given your sexuality every chance of flourishing. Initially, you're labelled a tease. You are obsessed with girls, but since you're convinced you're not yet 'post-pubescent', you chicken out when it comes to the act, and so leave them wanting more. When you turn seventeen – the year of the agonizingly slow dance – you risk a kiss. Then suddenly here you are: school holidays, the last days of August, the nights still warm, you are lying in the tall meadow grass. The English schoolgirl lying beside you is wondering why you still haven't slipped her the finger. You romanticize love, all the while masturbating furiously. Don't worry: once you get past the initiation, you will abandon the hopeless moors of romanticism and plunge headlong into pornography, which is just as much fun and will keep you company for the rest of your life. If you're lucky enough to spend a few months with the girl who took your virginity, you will very quickly end up trying out strange positions and find that the romantic feelings that attracted you to her fade into the middle distance. In fact, unrestrained romanticism leads directly to pornography. There is no happy medium. Nervous about your 'hazelnut syndrome', you also run the risk of looking gay. Whatever you are, you're a man of mystery: you don't talk to girls and you are reluctant to get undressed in changing rooms. After all, losing a testicle in a changing room is pretty embarrassing, especially if it is round and bounces away with a boing.

Now, here you are exploring the glorious byways of physical love. You're forty. It is five in the morning. You have drunk fifteen beers give or take. You're in a two-room apartment. Usually, any apartment you don't recognize at five in the morning will turn out to be filthy. This one is particularly so. There is evidence of exceptional grubbiness. There are panties and cigarette butts everywhere, two weeks' dirty dishes cunningly scattered around, etc. Even your own apartment has never been quite this bad. The last time you saw a place as messy and filthy as this it was your friend Toto's. As we know, he lives in a garret above his parents' apartment. He hasn't had a job in ten years. Whenever you talk to him about work, there is a mad, almost scary look in his eyes. You have spent endless nights boozing with him. You quite like him. But regardless of his pathological fault-finding with society, you feel he's letting himself go, that life is worth more than he is making of it. And you wouldn't like to be in his shoes. It is five o'clock in the morning. In your hand is a dirty glass full of white wine. You're not at Toto's place. In fact, you're not really sure where you are. You look blankly around this filthy room. The only thing missing, you realize, is a tramp. Look up a bit: there she is. Some strange woman has brought you back to her place. She is slumped on some sort of window seat. Her face is green. Maybe it has something to do with the colour of the walls. You probably look like a corpse yourself. Maybe, if she said she wanted you like a bitch in heat, if she threw herself at you, you might give in. After all, that's pretty much why you came home with her. She had interesting breasts but now they look strangely flabby. As it turns out, neither of you feels much like getting it on. She has drunk a dozen beers, she is having considerable trouble articulating. She tells you she is bisexual, that she works on and off. Lots of people are bisexual. There seem to be more and more of them around. Maybe it is a phase before the eventual disappearance of the sexes. Your years of unemployment flood back and you feel like throwing up. You were lucky to come through it. A sort of compassion wells up in your heart. But you're feeling sorry for yourself, too. When you get back to your place, you will jerk off to something on the Internet or rustle up some noodles. You feel almost happy. The evening could have turned out a lot worse. You could have woken up in some inexplicable bed beside some stranger with only one thing on her mind: getting you to leave. A woman you have only one thing in common with: being accident prone.

What is an electric toothbrush? Obviously, it is a device for vigorously massaging the clitoris, the labia minora and majora. Visit any department store, note the fiercely competitive market, the dizzying array of models on offer. As a regular visitor to sex shops, you will quickly notice a similar atmosphere in the electric toothbrush department: a number of connoisseurs lurk around for ages deciding what to buy. Choose a toothbrush with multiple speed settings. Feel free to choose the top-of-the-line model: the one where the main brush spins at the ideal speed, moving up and down in a thrusting motion, while a secondary brush vibrates. On the other had, the no-frills model will do just as well. The uncle first guessed the true purpose of this appliance one autumn night. An ordinary citizen of banal sexual tastes, he has just tied his partner to the bed with some belts. This is a woman he has been living with for some months. She is divorced. She has three children. The kids are staying at their father's. Like a lot of ordinary citizens, she likes to be tied up and whipped gently. In fact, she obviously picked out her bed with this in mind. One of her previous lovers gave her a long black whip. Having exhausted the pleasures of this device, the uncle finds himself running out of ideas. In the kitchen, he pours himself a large glass of Ricard and thinks. Suddenly he rushes to the bathroom and grabs the children's electric toothbrush. It is a pale-blue model with pictures of squirrels and bunny rabbits. The uncle's partner protests a little. She subsequently realizes that this little gadget will come in very handy for the rest of her days.

The uncle often finds himself attracted to older women; probably it is an indication of some unresolved Oedipus complex. Thanks to its technological wizardry, the Internet caters to even the most specialized sexual tastes. Its infamous branches can lead you to the very heart of your very own sexual labyrinth. In theory, by refining your search using successive pairs of criteria, it is possible to find the precise image around which your sexuality orbits: a fat, balding crone in chains sucking off a teenage Chechen boy in pink tights who is being fucked up the ass by a Breton spaniel in stockings and suspenders, which is grappling with a hairy Japanese man wearing a gigantic dildo whose ass is gaping from the ministrations of the barrel of an American tank, etc. This is called globalization. There is an obvious and terrible connection between the global and the infinitely small. It is perfectly possible that some day every cell in your body will be a consumer in its own right and multinational corporations will pitch products to them whether you like it or not. Just imagine every cell in your body – there are about a hundred thousand billion billion – equipped with a credit card. For now, just enjoy what is currently on offer in this magnificent marketplace of sexual frustration. Whatever else they offer, all porn sites have three more or less identical categories: *older women, grannies, housewives*. The third category creates the illusion of creeping into the privacy of someone's home where a bored housewife is just waiting for adultery: your virtual orgasm is coupled with the hazy pleasure of knowing you're a better lover than her husband. Obviously, these enticing cesspits are targeted at teenage boys with an incest fixation. These women, according to the hackneyed catchphrases used by such websites, are at 'the peak of their sexual maturity,'; they suck cock 'like you've never been sucked before'. And they're tried and tested to boot: 'to test them, we fuck them', the classy banner ads announce. In a nutshell, 'they love cock' above all else. A lot of these women are too young and not very convincing. You should never hesitate to complain about the quality of these websites, even the free sites. Never forget that as a customer, you have rights. In fact, you might consider suing peep shows, which just aren't as good as they used to be. On the Internet, if you're lucky, you will sometimes stumble on some perverted middle-class woman or one of the famous 'storytellers' from *The 120 Days of Sodom* with an ass as wrinkled and sagging as a dishcloth. As far as sex goes, de Sade was and always will be the undisputed inventor of the Internet.

Etc.

This is all very encouraging. All things considered, your *mens* is pretty much *sana*. You feel completely comfortable around women. You hold them in high esteem. You begin to write passages that incontestably are hymns to love. Judge for yourself . . .

The Petit Camp *experiment can be continued indefinitely. Take water clocks, for example. All water clocks follow the same design: the body of the spouse, whose volume has been measured, is suspended from a metal jib; with an electric drill, make a hole deep in the vagina; this process is known as deflowering; the thighs are held apart by a brace so that blood flow will be unhindered; the blood drips into a bowl . . . The most useful water clock can be used to time a boiled egg; the spouse takes four minutes to empty; the egg is eaten over the bowl; the toast soldiers are dipped in the blood . . . There is also the forty-hour water clock; the spouse bleeds out via a tiny hole over five days at the rate of eight hours a day, the Mechanic contemplates this futile flow . . . All of these procedures carried out on the body resemble bored noodling with a trombone . . .*

The Petit Camp *experiment can be continued indefinitely. Take the mechanical wife, for example. The movement of the spouse's loins is controlled thus: there is a gaping hole in the right shoulder where the clavicle has been replaced with the handlebar of a moped. The man should be strapped on in anticipation of top speeds. Opening and closure of the vagina together with lubrication require the insertion of a finger into the anus in order to reach a sort of hook. The wife's rigid tongue has two functions: cleaning the husband's nostrils or penetration of his oral cavity. (...)*

The Petit Camp *experiment can be continued indefinitely. Bodies may be stitched together two by two, three by three, four by four, etc. The most common configuration is the couple. Wire is used. A man and woman are stitched together face to face, groin to groin – lips sometimes joined in an everlasting kiss. The couple has a number of simple organic functions. The man's oesophagus, for example, has been sectioned and reattached to the woman's stomach; the woman digests a gruel which is poured into the man's beak; the man's bladder is attached to the tear ducts of the woman, he urinates; her eyes weep. The couple has a life expectancy of a couple of hours. Eventually, it is hoisted onto a gibbet. The couple turns slowly against the sky. The man gazes upon the woman welded to him. He urinates into her eyes.*

XVIII

How does a man go about becoming a loving part of a single-parent family? How do you go about rebuilding a happy blended family? Having seen a documentary about lions – wildlife programmes offer moral guidance particularly adapted to the modern world – the uncle has some good advice to offer, though he himself failed to solve this problem, having patently failed to use the correct technique.

The lion, apart from being king of the beasts – a description which should cause us to think hard and to adopt him as a role model – the lion, as I was saying, is a sensitive, affectionate creature. Lionesses kill in groups. The males fight among themselves or sleep. They spend more time sleeping than fighting. It is very hot. The females form prides. A male's sole purpose in life is to mount a takeover bid for one of these prides, so that he gets to reproduce and eat for free. Imagine two lone males, Maurice and Léon. They have spotted a thriving corporation of huntresses. Unfortunately, it already has a management team of two other males, who are thankfully more scrawny than they are. After

some brief, good-natured carnage, Momo and Léo take
control of the African co-operative. The females welcome
their new bosses philosophically, even though they're
obviously heartbroken, although the documentary
makes no mention of this. But two of the lionesses seem
worried. Koumba and Sara have already borne three
cubs to their former bosses. Though we don't know
their names, they're very young and terribly cute, even
though they are thugs in the making. The two lionesses
are nervous. They know what life is like here in the
savannah. Léo and Momo have no intention of becoming stepfathers. Lions, as is well known, are not terribly paternal. They have already spotted their
predecessors' offspring and are muttering to each other:
the cuddly toys over there, we'll sort them out. One of
the rules of wildlife documentaries is never to interfere
in the delightful balance of nature. In fact it is the cardi-
nal rule of wildlife documentaries. Except maybe in
exceptional circumstances if a cameraman is suddenly
bitten in the balls by a monkey. The voice-over is
detached, fatalistic, reassuring: Maurice and Léon cannot
allow Sara and Koumba's cubs to live, because they
would represent *overwhelming competition* for their
own offspring. It is all a question of balance. What
follows is not filmed in slow motion. This is unfortu-
nate. You can't quite work out what's happening. It all
happens too fast. Is that Momo or Léo ripping the head
off the first lion cub? Maybe you should write to the
channel and complain about the cursory manner in

which the scene was shot. Some time later, we see that Léon and Maurice have successfully become part of the pride, their chops are slightly red. Now they can devote themselves to the more pleasant and productive task of mating. For two or three days, the lion and lioness move away from the pride, who respect their privacy. They fuck every fifteen minutes and spend the rest of their time purring and indulging in lots of feline play-fighting. But Maurice and Léon's serenity is short-lived. A gang of four males prowls around the pride waiting for their moment to seize power. The battle will take place at night – the voice-over makes a point of paying tribute to the exceptional night vision of the lion, *six times more acute than that of man!* The average viewer, an adult male of about forty, is thinking that if he were in Léo and Momo's position, he would hightail it out of there and go bugger a zebra. Zebras aren't exactly in short supply in the savannah. But no. Momo and Léo stand firm. Night falls. We hear some top-quality roaring. Day breaks. The voice-over tells us that Léo has been killed, and we see some sort of hulk, mangy and alone, wandering off: it is Momo. The narrator waxes lyrical. Mortally wounded, Momo is searching for a place to die. We sympathize with Momo the child-killer. 'And he lies down for the last time' – (and indeed we see Momo lying down and, with great difficulty, licking a piece of red rag or, if you prefer, what remains of his left flank) – ' . . . Truly the lion is king of the beasts!' That's how it ends.

You might argue that the uncle hasn't actually
answered the original question of how to become part
of a single-parent family. Well, he has in part. Have a
bit of patience.

The uncle's second emotional suicide attempt occurs
one late-spring weekend at Whitsuntide, a long, wonderful disaster of a weekend. She didn't have custody of
the kids. Then they came back. It is true that the uncle
became fond of the kids and they of him. In fact –
must he come clean? – sometimes he still misses them.
But despite this, the uncle spent most of his time
wondering what he was doing mixed up in all this.
And sometimes he thinks that the lion's solution is a
good one: make a clean sweep.

XIX

Let us take a closer look at this second emotional suicide attempt.

Every February there is a week that heralds the spring, a sun-drenched parenthesis in the depths of winter. Every year the uncle watches for it, waits for it. For a few days, glorious sunshine settles over the city. The temperatures are more like what you would expect in May. You drink chilled rosé on strategically located terraces. Radiant bodies exchange smiles once more.

This is the perfect moment to commit adultery for the first time in your life, with a magnificent sense of abandon, a salutary impunity.

Okay, you have recently started taking antidepressants. *Adultera 500* is delicately beginning to break down your defences. You feel an irrepressible need for change.

The woman you have been living with is on holiday in Poitou-Charentes. The food is good there. There are pig farms and meadows there. Wherever there are pigs, nitrate levels rise. Children play. It rains. Wish you were here!

You are in Paris in the glorious sunshine. You go to see an exhibition of the Art of the Embalmer, feeling surprisingly full of life. You're with a slightly mad dark-haired woman you met a few days earlier. She is wearing a pair of wine-dark panties. She is a sculptor. She is tall, sensual, neurotic. Her mother is a psychiatrist, so is her father. She hates them both. You both go into raptures over all the resurrection-related exhibits: a skull with its eye sockets filled with pearls, a primitive head full of luxuriant straw, a Teutonic skeleton with a golden jaw grinning in opulent armour, etc.

Then the quiet café terrace, the tall bottle of rosé, a Tavel, alcohol content 14%. Florence drinks. She is a nervous, lively young woman completely in love with toxins. From the very first mouthful, your brain registers the alcohol content and opens in advance the pathways to minor liberties. The first sip trickles slowly between your synapses, and your eyes shine.

Florence invites you back to her place. She puts on some music. For the first time you discover the voice of Nina Simone. Nina once stayed in a hotel Florence was working in. There were drugs. And so, as Florence rolls a joint as vast as the uncertainty of love, you discover the first melancholy chords of 'Wild is the Wind'. For a split second you think about the woman you are about to betray. It doesn't last. Because now, *in this week that saved you*, you drink the dark, pungent lake – forgetfulness and excitement. You want to say that her ass against

your lips is not pornographic; just say that it was gener-
ously proportioned, more vast and more joyous than
a cave of dark seaweed. She suckled you with the
courage to break free and this is why you owe her
some sort of eternal gratitude.

But how or why did you so imperfectly abandon the
nitrate woman, your second emotional suicide attempt?

It is the beginning, the painful, somnambulistic
beginning of your fortieth birthday. You are writing
long-winded letters trying to get to the bottom of
things. The first is to Florence.

*How quickly bodies part, the glasses of rosé, the
sun's rays . . .*

*Here I am on the threshold of a great loneli-
ness, writing to ghosts.*

Naked.

*Stripped of the woman who was my guardian.
Stripped of the moments, the chasms, the cliffs,
the rivers and the towns. She loved the open road
and so we travelled.*

Why do I tell you these things?

*Life is a long series of leave-takings. We leave
people we will never stop loving.*

*I would like to have your body here tonight.
That body, barely thirty, its river, its response.*

Listen.

*Calm my fears of the looming loneliness, the
breaking apart.*

I cast my letters all over, like a hook without a rod. I am afraid of myself, of my freedom. Of the chasm into which I pour so much alcohol.

For the first time in my life, I am about to leave a woman. The decision I must make hurts me more than any decision I have ever made. Because it is has echoes of one I never made, one which has crushed my ability to decide: I never chose to leave my mother. And in leaving this woman I am reliving all the childish fears which prevented me from leaving that mother: the same feelings of guilt, the same fear of hurting, the same terror of standing alone in the cold light of day. Because to make such a decision, is, in the end, to stand completely naked before the other.

I have, in my life, avoided making decisions, I have hidden myself away. Lived in hiding, not for my own happiness, but to escape the gaze of a great inquisitor: my mother, not only as she is but as I have fashioned her within me.

A muzzle, a shot of anxiety, a tyranny that is, in the end, loveless. Because love, we hope, is a constant negotiation between two powers who wish to cleave to one another.

Etc.

Florence is surprised. She is not interested in your girlfriend. Nor in your mother. Her own is more than enough, 'a bitch who thinks about nothing except her career'. She broke up with the love of her life six months ago. She is not getting over it. Emotions scare her. You go and drink some more together. She gets appallingly drunk. She is thrown out of bars. She spends a handful of nights with you. She leaves at dawn while you're still asleep. There will be nothing more. Your first adulterous liaison is over. It has served its purpose.

To begin the telling of a love story with the adultery that clumsily ended it probably says something about the love story itself. We will call your second emotional suicide attempt Cruella, after *101 Dalmatians*. In *101 Dalmatians* Cruella wants a coat made of dog pelts. Fortunately, the cartoon has a happy ending: the puppies manage to save their skins. That is the moral of this wonderful film: sooner or later every puppy, even the 102nd, manages to save his skin.

Cruella was violent, sexual, self-centred, crude, and finally miserable. You loved her.

To tell a story of hate or of love is a difficult thing. You have to find an angle of attack, no matter how miserable and dishonest it is. Don't hesitate to introduce intermediaries. Let us imagine that, as you're writing this paragraph, the doorbell to your studio apartment rings. You set aside your beer, your joy. Through the peephole you see some creature, a woman of about seventy-five, brandishing a pair of slippers. There is a worn-out old man with her. He stands slightly back. The woman waves the giant slippers in front of the peephole. You are reluctant to open the door. 'Size

11! You just have to try them on!' Through the *judas,* you see the old man bow his head. With an immense weariness, you open the door. A torrent of words of no possible interest floods into the hall. A pointless, millennial unease permeates your studio. This tide of drivel, this metaphysical unintelligence, this thing you have struggled with since birth, this thing that refuses to die, that constantly returns to the fray, that will go to its grave understanding nothing, waves the new slippers under your nose. Because, she says, your old carpet slippers are obviously worn out. 'The suppliers,' she says, 'my vassals, have allayed my worries. They have imported this pair of fluffy prisons from cut-rate countries. We order you, dear embryo, to wear them.' You hastily throw your mother out.

And so we come to your second emotional suicide attempt. It is a Saturday evening, the eve of the long late-spring holiday weekend. You're out with John, an old publishing friend. John is sixty and looks fifty. He has always fancied boys and more recently young girls. He rules over his intellectual and sexual entourage like an aging tyrannical and benevolent father. In the bar he usually hangs out in, you get chatting to a friendly guy in a wheelchair. You talk, you drink profusely. John or someone else, suggests going to Satellites, a night-club of some sort 'where you dance and flirt forever'. You steer the wheelchair through the unctuous streets, you run, the guy is excited. You feel you are the Good Samaritan of the evening, your actions are virtuous and pure. It is summer. John, the old Dutch Jew, is having one of those conversations only he can have about editorial conspiracies against him, petty, small-minded France, situationists, etc. The only thing that matters is that he talks and exults endlessly. Here you are in the mayhem of Satellites. You turn heads with your wheelchair. A crowd warily gathers around you. You leave John and the guy in the wheelchair in the crowd. You go off for a drink.

A small, drunken, not particularly pretty woman is dancing with three random guys. Her eyes are closed, her smile oblivious. Your hunter's instinct immediately recognizes her as easy prey: the desperate, sexual, Saturday-night woman people exploit or defend, depending on their moral disposition, but defend always with the ulterior motive of taking advantage of her later. At the bar you sip your drink slowly. You toy with the glass in your hands, a tall glass of gin like a rigid organ of icy passion and ironic power. But alcohol won't be your compensation tonight, because you are more than a match for it. Out of the corner of your eye you watch the four bodies as they dance; it is like a game of billiards with the woman as the unimportant ball poked by the intoxicating thrust of shafts. Cruella lurches. You can tell she doesn't care about anything. Maybe she will go home alone, but at least the gaudy, cursed night will be over. She will masturbate and that will be that. On Sundays when her kids are staying with their father, Cruella usually wakes up with an atrocious hangover.

Sometimes there is a used condom by the bed. But she doesn't remember anything. You smile through the icy glass. She smiles back. The desperate are quick to recognize their own. You join the nuptial dance and, after some quick natural selection, you chase off these men with their twisted underpants to their silent, submissive curses. Because tonight, in your boundless, guiltless euphoria, you are the alpha male.

You ask Cruella to join you at the bar for a drink. She has the beautiful voice of a breathless angel, her lips are pure alcohol. She introduces you to her friend. Annie is single and forty. She has shocking bags under her eyes. She and Cruella always go clubbing together. She goes clubbing all the time in hopes of meeting a man, but she always goes home alone. She is skinny and sad. She has no children. As they get closer to forty, women start to worry. By forty-two they panic. Men avoid them like the plague, finding them tiring and depressing. They're obviously just looking for someone to get them pregnant. Men only want to fuck or if they decide they do want a son and heir, they go for younger women. It is only human. The smart ones shit out a kid in a blind panic, a terrible genetic hysteria, on the pretext that they will soon be unable to ever have a baby. In fact, the first thing they should do is take a long, hard look at the reasons they're still childless at such an advanced age. Annie sizes you up disappointedly, but her technique is all wrong. Cruella always gets the men she goes for. She has long since satisfied her maternal urges. She has three children. All she wants now is to fuck or to feel less alone. Nothing more. Men can smell this and move in on her with heavy glands and suppressed rage.

It is four o'clock in the morning. Cruella is completely drunk and doesn't feel up to driving. Annie, who is kind and has no boyfriend and nothing better to do, takes the wheel. You make polite conversation. Annie turns out to be a cleaning lady. She lives in a studio apartment in Aubervilliers. It is not big, but it has a loft bed. She'd like to change her career, become a care assistant or go to university, but she never finished high school. She does cleaning work for old people and helps Arabs fill out their government forms. If she had the money, she'd sign up with a dating agency. She sometimes replies to lonely hearts ads, but the men are always disappointing. Cruella slumps forward, half asleep. She jerks upright every thirty seconds, then dozes off again. She looks like a dishrag attached to the seatbelt. You are completely comfortable with such disastrous nights. From the back seat of the Peugeot 309 you chat amiably, considerate and sensitive to these humble lives. When you get to the street Cruella lives on, you are overjoyed. It is a street you know like the back of your hand, because this is where your ex-wife Jojo, aristocratic Jojo, Jojo of the silken hands, practised furiously and scornfully as a medical secretary. Destiny is brewing up a terrible night in a cauldron of cackles.

Do not hesitate to be sordidly Christian in your account of what happened that night. After all, you were drunk. You don't remember all the positions you tried out on the debauched body.

But first Cruella must be removed from the 309. Annie watches. The removal is as long and ludicrous as the descent from the cross. For a split second it crosses your mind that the Romans must have hired removal men to take Christ down. The deposition of Christ and the removal of an alcoholic from a Peugeot 309 is a job for professionals. A tiny drunken woman is as heavy as a dead god. Not that professionals are perfect. The removal men who shifted Christ probably made some practical mistakes. One of them hasn't checked his grip and drops the Nazarene to voluble swearing from his colleagues on that crimson Sabbath evening. Or maybe in a post-mortem reflex Jesus let rip a huge last fart, causing a recoil that made the ladder wobble and himself to fall. There are lots of possible scenarios. In certain versions of the *Pietà*, the women surrounding the man fallen from the *forked tree* seem very distraught, and they have good reason: Christ's shorts are torn and dirtied from the fall caused by the ham-fisted removal men. The altarpiece by Van Neuroosis gives pride of place to these shorts. From one of the side panels, the disciple whom Jesus loved points to the shorts. In the central panel, Mary sews up her son's breeches with a reproachful expression. Another Dutch artist of the period, Van Psychoosis,

portrayed another aspect of this scene. On the panel
on the left, the Mother of God is on all fours, feverishly scrubbing her son's body with a sponge. In the
right-hand panel, she polishes the cross with a tea
towel before taking it home to put with the other
relics. In fact, legend has it that she has a box in
which she keeps Jesus's first teeth, even his umbilical
cord. She believes it is her duty. In fact, in a dark
corner of the central panel Van Psychoosis portrays
these relics: the shrivelled and desiccated cord is
symbolically placed next to a skull. But let us get back
to Cruella, patron saint of prostitutes and alcoholic
beverages. While you're awkwardly trying to get her
out of the car, you take advantage of the state she is
in to confirm the *thong theory*. Because a girl like this
has to be wearing a red thong, the dreamlike g-string,
the loincloth of indecency, the razor-sharp underwear
of the crucified, etc. So you hike up her skirt and feel
around, the incestuous nylon, the soft gates of Saint
Peter, embassy of tropical rainstorms, with a seedy and
Faulknerian seriousness. Then you steady the body
awkwardly against the bonnet and close the car door.
She falls. You half expected this. But drunkenness has
relieved you of all awareness of other people's suffering. As she falls, her hair lashes you like red thorns.
Now she is sitting on the pavement. She spends a long
time laughing and vomiting wine.

You carry her unsteadily. You wish you were a butcher.
Butchers carry sides of beef over their shoulders. Their

shoulders are white and serene. Giggling to yourself, you eventually manage to get into Cruella's apartment with great difficulty. She runs to the toilet to throw up. Annie offers to make an omelette, giving you plenty of time to explore the living room, which your friends will later describe as pervaded by 'extraordinary violence'. It is a large, slightly curved room. The colour of the walls is something like *egg yolk*, the floor is *spinach*. But the first thing that strikes you is the omnipresent red, a dark red usually referred to as *oxblood*, but for which you would like to propose the following names: *abattoir red, vampire red, ogre red, furious red, psychotic red, homicidal red, the red of a night of rape, the red of wine spilt and vomited, the red of childbirth in a backstreet clinic, torture red, tragedy red, Cruella red*. There is a host of dark-red objects and furniture scattered about the room like screams: sofa, chairs, vases, armchairs, lamps – reflections of the essential soul, the bloody and despotic soul of Cruella – Cruella your second emasculator, whom you chose that night in the certain knowledge that you will finally be able to carry out – if only by proxy – the act you have dreamed of and postponed for so long, a liberating matricide. This, curiously, is the role Cruella will play in the subconscious shaping of your destiny – Cruella will be your mother in effigy, callous, selfish, murderous. Because the time has come and you have to go back through hell. You stare at the black, wrought-iron curtain rods; their twisted, barbed shape

– a shape you have never seen before – reminds you of the spikes on which the souls of the damned are roasted. There is a dried-up, shrivelled plant, a dying weed in a large pot the colour of abortion. Lastly, you notice the complete lack of books.

Your autopsy of the living room is rudely interrupted by Annie asking you to go and check on Cruella, who has been in the toilet for over a quarter of an hour. She can't hear any vomiting. She is a little worried. You go about the task joyfully. You open the door. Perched over the smell of urine, wine, and half-digested meat sits Cruella. She is half asleep, her head slumped forward, her skirt hitched up, her thong and tights down. She insults you half-heartedly as you help her to sit up – *leave me the fuck alone, go home arsehole, etc.* – as she tries to get your trousers off and suck on your cock, which is comatose after fifteen gins. You eagerly slip her thong and her tights up those slim, nervous thighs. You have barely stepped out of the toilet when she asks you to escort her back to that pleasant place where, in heaving shudders, she vomits up the *marchand de vin* sauce. In the distance, Annie says, 'Shit!' The omelette has been completely burnt and she has ruined the 'skelet'. You take this opportunity to demonstrate to Annie and the vomit factory the extent of your learning. Because a *skelet*, Annie, a *skelet* – as opposed to a skillet or a skill-set – is a word derived from old Dutch which means a mummy or skeleton. 'Must be great to be a teacher . . .' says Annie dreamily, wiping Cruella's lips with a sponge dipped in vinegar.

Annie heads off for the towers, the standing coffins, of Aubervilliers.

And that's when you remember the ring road, the terrible boredom you felt when you were twenty-seven, the depressing carpets, your colleague's empty breasts. It was a desolate time. At night – as a treat – you would buy sauerkraut from the clubfoot Italian on Rue Doudeauville. The tubs of sauerkraut were black and steaming. You were alone. You were pining for the woman you loved when you were twenty-six, the uncompromising, sleepless love you shared in a sloping district, in gently apocalyptic apartments, the tall, shrill girl who even today, if she is not dead, is probably still desirable and heartbreaking.

You like the almost rundown suburbs, the poor crammed together with geometric precision. Annie drives off in some rough-and-ready car. Here you are, alone with Cruella. It is a late-spring holiday weekend at Whitsuntide.

You spent two days in bed drinking and laughing. Cruella seemed happy and so did you. She hadn't met a stable guy for six months. She had lived with her previous lover for two years and then he'd left her. He wanted a child. But the father of those she already had had caused her too much pain. So she said no. Today, you understand why he decided to leave her. The holiday weekend is wonderful. You remember the tinkle of ice cubes in pastis. You would go and seek out miraculous things in the sun-drenched kitchen.

By Sunday, at about 6:00 p.m., the woman was asleep, getting her strength back. While she was sleeping, you wrote a sort of poem. You'd found a new job. You'd started to write again, to love again. The words came out like pulsing blood:

The bull resists O ballerina

Eye altar of sacrifices
I was central.

My hands tremble
I back up towards you like fearful blood

My Distant One
My Wanderer
Compass orphaned by the poles

An immortal beast longs to die

Anguish clot of joys and words
                    multipolar

They come to my door with drums

I have found the motherlode

And so you spent two days together. You discovered you had other things in common besides alcohol. Cruella worked in the same department as your brother. Her mother lived in the town where your father was born. Every summer she went back there with her kids. Then she'd head south staying in tents, chalets and mobile homes in holiday villages with views over valleys, rivers, reservoirs, in the Tarn, the Dordogne, etc. In time, you will go to these places with them, feeling a little out of place, and increasingly convinced that there is no such thing as a happy second family. You will go to theme parks that make your head spin. You will think that being a father means wanting to be a child, dozing quietly and waiting for night and the sensual body of your wife. But for all that, you felt a sort of happiness, the gridlocked roads, the rowdy children. Under copper-coloured fir trees, near the end of the trip, you'd turn round to give them sweets and affectionate whacks. You probably loved them. The car is a metaphor for life. Once, you sat in the back seat. Your father was thrilled to have a new car. You glided around carefree in the white Citroen DS. The cornering was emetic. Now you sit in the front seat. There is nothing you can do about it. Families forcibly remind you of this obvious fact. When you're in the front seat, you have to wear a mask, a fake smile. In the back, you don't have to yet. Cruella was happy. You would arrive in wooden villages in the evenings. The kids would race down and jump into swimming pools, still warm in the last rays of sunshine.

You discovered these utilitarian spaces with a sort of ecstasy: the bunk beds, the veranda with a plastic table in the shade of the pine trees, the lake in the distance. You always loved tiny spaces.

June goes by pleasantly enough. Cruella is drinking in moderation. Every night she takes a Stilnox. You meet her children. The youngest girl opens the bedroom door every morning and climbs into bed between you. Jealous and curious, she comes to check out the new man who is sleeping with her mother. She lifts up the sheet and looks at your penis. The oldest boy is twelve and wets the bed. He is intelligent and dyslexic. The third child is autistic or something. He stubbornly believes that two and two make five. He often gets nosebleeds, usually in the middle of the night. He is a ten-year-old Christ, the suffering centre of the family, its most obvious symptom. You wish the youngest girl weren't asthmatic. Unfortunately, she is. The children visit psychologists, allergists, speech therapists, psychiatrists, witches, etc. Cruella spends her time driving them back and forth. You slowly discover the everyday joys of a stable family. There is spaghetti every night. There is happiness too. But the happiness doesn't show up in clinical trials. Your mother would like Cruella. 'She is not afraid of hard work, that woman,' she would say. 'She has three children and she is a nurse.' After a while the children come to accept you, although they still miss her previous boyfriend who loved them for two years. Their father, apparently, is brilliant but mad. He lives like a hermit in the suburbs. He could not cope with the breakup. When Cruella told him that she was leaving, he tried to strangle her in the garden but stopped himself just in time. Cruella showed you the spot under the night-flowering tree where the deed was done. She is suing him over the children. He wants full custody. He half-heartedly protests as part of some fathers' rights group. He lives with a divorced taxi driver and goes to a chess club. The taxi driver would like to sleep with Cruella under the night-flowering trees, apparently, as some sort of sexual plot. The father is having trouble coping. He often forgets to pick up the kids. The children stand there, dressed and ready, holding their schoolbags, waiting. Weeks go by with no word from him. The battle between them is wearing Cruella out. She often wishes he were dead. He watches films, she says, porn films in which people are brutally tortured. Scenes in bathtubs with razors. He sometimes goes to a prostitute. Even Cruella, who is fascinated by sexual torture, thinks this is unhealthy. All she wants is for someone to tie her up, blindfold her, and tenderly thrash her with the long black whip that was given to her by her ex-lover. In the end, you start to enjoy it. You bite her earlobes, she pinches your nipples. You're both sexually frustrated, this is your common ground, it is probably the only thing you have in common apart from alcohol. You long for tenderness, but hatred, with its little cruelties, is not so bad. Later you will buy two interesting gadgets from a sex shop. You gleefully haggled with the salesman late into the night, discussed the advantages and disadvantages, asked his advice. In the end, he gave you a special price for buying both. Toto, who was with you at the time, *that charming boy* Toto, Toto who is living off minimum benefits, was shocked by this indecent purchase. One of the gadgets is an elaborate vibrator: it is a black plastic scorpion that can be attached by a suction cup to the belly of your beloved. The segmented tail is introduced into the anus while the vibrating body or cephalothorax, massages the vulva. The speed is controlled by a small remote control fitted with two AAA batteries. It is completely useless. You'd be much better off using the electric toothbrush demonstrated in chapter XVII.

Now, suddenly it is the holidays, the sweet July holidays, a new hell. The weather is beautiful, you and Cruella have been together about a month. The father takes the kids away to some unspeakable mountain. Doses of alcohol and Stilnox suddenly soar. Cruella can't hold her drink. They say alcohol reveals what a person is really like. This is a rule that needs to be qualified. People who have had too much to drink usually display the same traits, to a greater or lesser extent. Calm people become slightly confrontational. Violent people become enraged. We all have claws, short or long, sheathed or shown. Alcohol frees them, magnifies them, and turns them towards the outside world. Those who constantly poison themselves in greater-than-human quantities have a boundless violence and a pain within them which is *inextricably related to love*. Cruella's claws, vicious even when she is sober, become monstrous in drunkenness, a dark, sexual drunkenness. She would lash out at you with the violence of the womb, of a mother of three whose only ties to this world had been severed. Her children are the only things she ever created, but they are also the result of a lifetime of mistakes: a father who abandoned her; an alcoholic, absent mother; a botched childhood, and the inevitable consequence, the slowly escalating hatred, a hatred that would compensate her, calculated according to the market value of her misery – as the market for misery rises, the hatred, Cruella's attractive hatred, becomes exorbitant – then her flight into sex, catastrophic love affairs, an ill-chosen husband, the triple knot of children of whom only the first was conceived in an unhoped-for surge of happiness, the other two, as often happens, born of some crazy attempt to save the marriage, then the breakup, head above water for a moment, the two years with her lover, another breakup, the terrible week in February when Cruella realized he had left her, the months of sex and booze, and now a glimmer of light in this cycle, a new window, hope mingled with hate: you.

Love is two violent forces coming together, a struggle in mud and gold. You made your vows to each other late one wild July night. You had thrown her out of bed, she was lying on the floor, her hair wet, because in an attempt to stop her humiliating cruelty you had thrown a whole jug of water over her. A couple of hours earlier, at an impromptu party, she had deliberately taunted you, dancing with other men and pressing herself against them. Her children had gone away that same day. She was drunk. You had tried to drag her away from the party by force. You had made a scene. She had bitten your hand so deeply you could still see the teeth marks. Now she was lying on the floor, on the threadbare carpet. You suddenly told her that you loved her, that she had *won*. She was drunk but the words still brought a glimmer of amazement to her eyes.

Her lips parted.

And suddenly you imagined men taking her roughly, in a voyeuristic double penetration, in the thrilling secretions, in a moment verging on eternity.

For maybe she was no more than an image fashioned out of your own mud.

You lingered in the gutters of love.

One evening, you lived out this breathless fantasy. You wanted to see her taken by another man. This classic fantasy unquestionably contains several elements: latent homosexuality, the desire to be humiliated, incest by proxy, a holy trinity . . . The reality was sordid and comical. You cannot live out a fantasy. The man could barely get it up.

Sex is probably the only means we have found, however pitiful, to say something about love.

July passes, violent, alcohol fuelled, bathed in the

colour red. She keeps bottles lined up under the sink. You hide them. She begs you to tell her where you have hidden them. You give in, for you too are thirsty for violence. There is tenderness too.

Calm is restored when the children come home. She takes them to Lorient. You are summoned there a week later. It is the beginning of August.

All families have secret wounds, stifled screams. Cruella's family was no exception to this rule. What was different here was that people talked about their suffering out loud. Everyone drank exquisitely, the sisters as much as brothers-in-law, the mother, the mother's lover, etc.

As soon as you arrived in the oceanic public housing, you demanded vast doses of alcohol. Your reputation as a drinker had preceded you. You did it justice.

From all over Lorient and the provinces of France, people had flocked to see Cruella's new boyfriend – Cruella, the eldest in the family, the most damaged, the girl who came home every summer, who was as dependent on her mother as she was on booze, though every year she swore she'd cut down the dose.

With age, the mother was mending her ways. She was trying to win back from her children, if not their wounded affection, their unattainable respect, then at least some sort of forgiveness. She would cry when the holidays were over, when the time came to say good-bye, when her daughters were leaving. The apartment was empty. She drank all day long. From the moment you got there you pinched her cheeks, flattered her bum. It is always easier with other people's mothers. You called her *Mamie*. You had access to her *private stock*. In one evening you became the favourite brother-in-law in this humble, joyful, uneducated crowd.

You spent a week there, it was a wonderful holiday, like a sort of childhood with beaches and swimming – and alcohol, to boot. Sitting on the beach among these simple folk you believed in love; even Cruella was more affectionate than she would ever be again. The children played far off under keen and lustful supervision. The sisters chatted happily. There was laughter, ice cream and brioche. You were practically a father.

Lorient is an ugly town. The postwar rebuilding is dreadful for the most part. There is an old German submarine base, harbours, fish factories, suburbs and, thankfully, beaches. It is a ghost town. Winter is terrible here. But in early August there is the Inter-Celtic festival with fairgrounds, french fries and fireworks. It is the town's only attraction. Celts from all over Europe flock there. For ten days they drink themselves into a stupor in their kilts and beards. They dance round in circles in community halls. They eat crêpes. The Celts haven't evolved one whit in four thousand years. In fact, the extreme right loves them. To cap it all off, they come from Germany. Celtic music hasn't evolved either, though there have been some attempts. What you might call cutting-edge Celtic. A couple of electric guitars wailing away with the Breton bagpipes.

It is all still terribly folksy. The Lorient Inter-Celtic festival was Cruella's chief contribution to the broadening of your cultural horizons. She made pertinent critical observations: 'It is not as good as last year,' she said over and over.

Then you headed south. You hadn't planned it, but you were in love. Cruella had booked a magical week on the Costa Brava, in a tower of approximately two thousand rooms, *just two steps from the beach*. This was to be her real holiday. She brought thongs for the dances. You spent your very first night under canvas on the shores of a reservoir. You made love in the tent surrounded by the kids. They were supposedly asleep. Still, it was embarrassing. Then came Spain, the hideous coast, the tower-blocks, the tourist traps. Everything was full. There was no room for you. A room for four people is not a room for five. There are moral standards for packing people in. Even the elevators were jammed. You waited endlessly. Herds of people arrived, headed for the feeding troughs or the teeming swimming pool. You slept illicitly in her room. You made love amongst the children again, more violently this time. The autistic one got a nosebleed at two in the morning. The next morning, a little sadly, you headed back to Paris.

Etc.

Your first breakup from Cruella came after approximately twenty-two months. Breaking up with Cruella is something that requires patience. You have to gradually

put in place all the necessary logistical resources: weekly
panic attacks, psychologist, antidepressants, adultery, etc.
You spend the first six months in love. *You truly loved
her and your love swept her off her feet.* In the second
six months comes disillusionment. Your agreeable family
life of theme parks, daily spaghetti, weekends at her
sister's, Saturdays at Ikea, sexual acts involving multiple
bite marks – this blissful life is not enough to compensate for your growing conviction that she does not love
you. Cruella explains that she loves you *in her own way.*
She even gives you a Christmas present. You agree in
advance that the gift will cost no more than a thousand
francs, but when, trembling with excitement, you go
with her to the department store, the VCR the sales-
person recommends she buy for you costs twelve
hundred francs. So Cruella asks you for a cheque for
two hundred francs. You have your first panic attack
after a year. It is true you're naturally a person of nervous disposition and you have been drinking heavily. To
those readers who have forgotten, a typical panic attack
lasts for a period of two hours during which you think
you are going to die. Soon, you're having two or three
a week. You put on a brave face in front of Cruella's
kids, but you feel as though you are floating in space.
The spaceship is getting farther and farther away. You
are alone in the void. There is no one to help you.
Cruella silently waits for you to leave her. Your panic
attacks become more frequent. All the alarm signals
are flashing. But you don't want to see. The rest we

know: all you need now are a psychiatrist, some anti-depressants, a little adultery and time.

When you move out, she brings in a substitute. It's Toto, *that charming boy* Toto. It's all very petty. But you are beginning to feel alive again. It suits you fine. She takes him to the Inter-Celtic Festival. Unfortunately within three months she wears him out. So she summons you. Unfortunately, you go running back. You re-enlist for about six months. Then there are other breakups, and shorter tours of duty.

What is the moral of this tale?

The doorbell to your studio rings. You set aside your beer, your joy, etc. This is another intermediary. This time, through the peephole, you see an octopus. The octopus is about 165 centimetres tall and is clutching *the exhausted old man* in one of her tentacles. You go to the kitchen and get an axe before opening the door. The beast, overjoyed, makes herself at home in your hall. Her eyes are green and incestuous. In her tentacles, she is clutching, in no particular order: a shopping trolley, a box of suppositories, your umbilical cord, your first school essay, your death certificate, a meal cooked with abyssal loving care, some ironed shirts, etc. The octopus tries to grab you. You signal to the old prisoner. He doesn't see you. You scream. He doesn't hear you. So you start to hack off the tentacles. But they grow back. The octopus brandishes her tears, her certificate of madness, a pair of emasculated brothers, a box of aspirin, frozen steaks, kisses, bits of the old father, etc. You slash at her with the conceptual axe, but it is no good. It all grows back: your alcoholism, your fucked-up love life, your suppressed loathing. Suddenly, you realize you're alone in the hall, staring at yourself in a mirror. You have the face of an octopus, your arms have been hacked off.

These days, Cruella has joined a dating agency and is taking antidepressants. She goes dancing and plays cards. The agency she is registered with is full of old men looking to fuck. Apparently, the divorcées stare spitefully at each other. Cruella is also taking tango lessons. Tango is her new obsession. It takes up every weekend. Cruella dreamed of being happy. She runs through the night, more and more covered in bruises. The unutterable name of love is on the tip of her tongue, then, like so many, she disappears into the crowd. Some day, she will tell you that she nearly became a prostitute, that if it weren't for her children she'd be dead. The tragedy of women is perhaps greater than that of men. They are the unhappy passages though which we are born. As time goes by, they are increasingly lonely. They go off by themselves and have children and then ask damaged men to step into the shoes of the fathers who have walked out on them. They rear their litter by themselves with animal tenacity. Their happiness expectancy is about fifteen years.

You can see her slim figure, her nervous, staccato walk and every place she ever dragged you to. Stubbornly she dragged you to campsites overlooking the ancient waterfalls of France. These twisting, venerable waterfalls spoke to you of utopian pleasures, of the simple happiness of aquatic peoples.

You can see her, shadowy and uncertain, torn between love and revenge.

The people we have most failed in a lifetime of failures haunt us. Our consolation is to know or at least to hope that they are happier now.

XX

We cannot blame all of our problems on our families. The family, after all, is simply a microcosm of society, and obviously society is not motivated by the happiness of its members. But since, firstly, most of us don't have the necessary skills to undertake a detailed analysis of a complex society, and secondly, we should take the easy option of looking for the causes of our suffering outside ourselves, so the *family hypothesis* instinctively occurs to us – and we should trust our instincts. When he thinks about his nighttime world, the uncle finds it peculiar that his dreams are constantly populated by members of his family lined up before him like ominous chessmen, while he always turns up in his dreams as a guilty, frustrated child dressed in ridiculous clothes that are far too small for him. The family hypo-thesis, like all hypotheses, only becomes interesting if taken to its logical conclusion. You only risk being in the wrong in the short term or being hypocritical. Whatever happens, you will have loosened up a great deal of frustration. Give yourself an enemy, make your enemy the cause of all your suffering: at worst, you will end up hurting yourself and in doing so gain some insight into your misfortune or at least some relief. Blame your enemy for all the regular, painful things your feeble willpower cannot stop you from doing: your alcoholism, your pathetic sex life, your constant depression, your panic attacks, your destructiveness – blame it all on your enemy and absolve yourself for a moment.

Two types of family seem particularly effective in the amount of suffering they cause their members. There are probably others, but let us concentrate on these two. Model one: Bruno's mother abandoned him at birth. She is still alive. He knows where she lives, Paradoxically, being abandoned is what has pushed him in his increasingly brilliant career. His hatred and his need for acceptance will never be satisfied. In fact, hatred is the wellspring of success. Bruno is miserable as a dog. He fathered a child and ended up abandoning him. His child, in turn, will grow up to hate him. This reproductive rule is borne out by Anna's experience. Her father walked out on his family when she was six months old, went off to sow his pitiful wild oats all over the world. She has half-brothers and -sisters in four or five different countries. She has never met any of them. She is beautiful, intelligent and completely miserable. At thirty-two, she decided to recreate the wonderful family model she had. She got pregnant by a man she had an affair with. In her own words, 95 percent of her life is now devoted to her child. Being the repository of 95 percent of a mother's life does not predispose one to happiness.

The second family model is the one the uncle endured. It is similar to a life sentence. In this model, one of the parents wields absolute control over every member of the family without a flicker of intelligence or kindness. This parent passes down her fear of others, fear of sex, fear of life, and a number of other heartwarming virtues. The second parent doesn't get involved. The official reason for this self-effacement is that he just wants a quiet life. This is a lie. In fact, he himself has been completely dominated since childhood and knows no way out other than to throw himself back into the lion's den. He has never argued with the tyrant. This means that, without outside help, you in turn will either let yourself be dominated by mediocre people or you will try to dominate other people without a flicker of intelligence or kindness. You would probably be better off in a family where the parents pass the time ripping each other to shreds, because they will eventually divorce or they will teach you how to manage suffering democratically. The family model the uncle endured may or may not produce talented children. But, whatever else they may be, they will be miserable and their talent will be nothing more than a hanged man's erection.[1]

The following story will make it clear how farcical this model is. The uncle is twenty-two years old. For

---

[1] The uncle, who has often fallen in love with impossible women, once composed a sort of plea to one of these women. She was twenty years younger than him. The plea ended thus:

the first time in his life, he stayed out all night without telling his mother. At 7 a.m., the worried mammal starts to phone his friends. One of his friends puts forward the theory of a prolonged coitus. He gives her the young lady's name. Immediately, the young lady's phone rings. On the uncle's instructions, the young lady – who finds the whole thing very funny – tells the mammal that her cub isn't there. Panic sets in. The mammal wakes up the whole city. As bad luck would have it, she stumbles upon another mammal, a frustrated idiot who married a doctor. The two women get along like a house on fire. 'My dear lady,' suggests the second mammal, 'if I were in your shoes, I'd be ringing the police stations and the hospitals by now!' It is at this point that the uncle, who has been warned of this new turn of events, phones his darling mother, who spends a full ten minutes hauling him over the coals. This tongue-lashing is certainly the result of her justifiable worry. But there is something else: the mammal is convinced that her cub has spent the night with a prostitute. The phrase crops up more than once: 'You

---

I arrived with the peoples of my suffering
And the exhausted embryo

I have weight and I have needs

Family fearful wall
Cancerous glove
Strangler of cathedrals

were off with some whore, admit it!' She ends the conversation with a terrifying threat: 'Your father wants to see you. You are to meet him at his office at five o'clock.' The young lady is in fits of laughter. But she is already carefully planning the breakup. At five o'clock, the uncle goes to his father's office. His father is a kind, circumspect man. He tells his son not to be too angry with his mother, she has been under a lot of pressure lately, etc. A lot of feeble fathers resort to this line of argument. He concludes with an exquisite line: 'Your mother is a fine woman . . . and an excellent cook!' On this last point, at least, he is wrong. But this phrase sums up thirty years of his life.

Is it better to be abandoned by your mother or to have one who still thinks of you as a permanent offshoot of her ovaries, her very own second home? The uncle is not very fond of mothers. Especially those who don't work or who pretend to work. He's not the only one. A middle-class mother who smells of bleach because she spends her life frantically doing housework is certainly respectable, but what she conveys to you is an inexhaustible boredom for life. There are probably people who are not very fond of fathers. You can even be fond of neither. It is something in which we're guided by our own experience. It is difficult to love someone who is authoritarian, self-centred, constantly dissatisfied and who has built her happiness upon her utter disregard for yours. The uncle is frequently irritated to hear sons making booming declarations of love to their mothers. To listen to them, you would think mothers were goddesses filled with affection and selflessness. Many of them are mammals only interested in having babies. Their one regret is that, after a certain age, they can no longer bear children and they lose the control they once had over the children they have. Love had nothing to do with their choice of a mate. Their primary consideration was security or social status. Some have simply replicated what they experienced as children, something they have never succeeded in overcoming: disaster.

Let us take a look at an extreme case as it is televised. The programme is devoted to the family, but it looks like a wildlife documentary. We are introduced to a mother of fifteen children. She is sixty years old. She is plump, utterly selfish and prodigiously authoritarian. She is a dominant female. Her husband died, probably from exhaustion. Why did she have fifteen children? If it were because she was ignorant about contraception, you might feel sorry for her. But that is not her reason. One of a family of fourteen children, she and one of her brothers were abandoned by their mother. So she set herself a challenge, she set out to prove to her negligent mother that it was possible to bring fifteen children into the world and not abandon one of them. Nice motive. People who stubbornly insist on propagating the species should think long and hard about what they're doing. Reproduction is like a game of Old Maid in which each generation palms off on the next a card that nobody wants. Where is it written that life is so wonderful that we continually have to force it on others? Why, just because life has appeared on this planet, does it have to carry on? 'You have to understand,' the fat old sow explains, 'I had to have one more than she did, and not abandon a single one of them!' Did you think you were conceived out of love? Think again: as often as not you are the result of selfish, petty-minded scheming. It is true that there are more extravagant schemes. Let us look at a Palestinian mother. She procreates prolif-ically and convinces her sisters and her cousins to do likewise. They bear sons who will blow themselves up in suicide bombings. Every son is worth about twenty-five thousand dollars. That is the price Iraq pays for every martyr. A mother like this is very proud to mass-produce murderers who will die for her, for Palestine and for an ignoble god. Her husband seems almost sympathetic. He regrets the death of his eldest boy. His eldest son was a student, he could have served his country in some other way. The father points to one of his younger sons: 'Why not him?' But let us get back to the sow. Her plan has been a complete success. Most of her children, especially the boys, live with her. We see a group of emasculated forty-somethings stand-ing on a stage smiling adoringly at their mother. The girls seem to have put up more of a struggle. But the eldest girl seems worn out from forty years of fighting. The tyrant doesn't really understand the tactful questions being put to her. The interviewer expresses surprise that her sons are still living with their mother when they have girlfriends and children of their own. 'Oh yes,' the bitch crows, 'some of them even got divorced just so they could come back and live with me! They weren't happy with those wives of theirs . . .' The presenter keeps smiling, remains diplomatic. She refers to them as the 'astonishing tribe'.

People often say that the most devastating loss is the death of a child. The uncle believes this. He has seen it happen among people truly moved by love. But he cannot help but think that surviving your children is sometimes a sort of obscure victory. For some people, being the only survivor of a disaster is like a crowning achievement. The uncle cannot help but think that his mother will cling to life at all costs for as long as she can. This lust for life would be laudable if it weren't completely involuntary.

To face down a tyrant means nothing. In time, the victims eventually come to agree with the tyrant. It is a system that does not tolerate opposition. The uncle's family is peopled by pitiful shadows he could never possibly count on for support. He too has taken sides. He thinks he's come through things better than the others. But it is a long battle and the price to be paid is high. Waging a constant war on your own family, feeling utterly disowned, cutting the most basic human ties, these things are horribly painful, and there is no guarantee that when your suffering is over you will be free.

Anyone who thinks families act out of love should think again. A family is an exercise in domination. As in every group, you will find people who want to dominate others. They get no satisfaction out of life. To begin with it was just a mother or father. But the dismal tyrants procreated. Maybe what you find most depressing about the system that made you suffer is that it carries on with pathetic regularity. From generation to generation, you see the same submissive smile or the same macabre rictus on the faces of your nearest and dearest. There will always be some brother or sister, some niece or nephew who spends their every waking moment putting you down or trying to get one up on you. These days, you're not in the front line any more. You watch the whole thing wearily from a distance. And when your parents die, the last thing binding you to this family will melt away like sand in the evening tide. You might feel a bit sad. But you will feel as if, at long last, the holidays have begun.

You let people push you around because you thought they loved you. They fobbed you off with the old 'love' routine in the paradise of cheap trash they call childhood. They have got you well trained. Just listen to your family sit in judgement over others: all the arrogance, the facile nitpicking, the constant paranoia. They talk about people who are infinitely better human beings than they could ever be as if they were cockroaches. Why should they spare you? Because you are family? For as long you believe you are loved, you will be dominated by dull, narrow-minded people. Dispense with this last illusion and the true face of your family appears. Do you find them interesting, distinguished? They're mediocre and frightened. Their delusions of grandeur are grotesque. From generation to generation, their names are inscribed in the registers of the most prestigious schools as on a memorial to the dead.

You were raised in a maximum-security prison, away from other people. Even your closest relatives are strangers to you. It is true they passed on certain intellectual qualities, but these are nothing more than heartless reflexes. It has taken you longer than most to become human – a process your family had no hand in – you are not even sure whether you have succeeded. Some vital part of you will always be missing. To you, people are abstract ideas. You are not genuinely interested in them. And when you try to empathize, it is intellectually, not emotionally. You cry out for love. You whimper because you can't find it. But in reality, you want nothing to do with love. The affection lavished on you seems vaguely threatening to you. You pushed away every person who loved you and, in due course, they grew tired. You pushed them away precisely because they loved you. You have an almost primordial need to be with people who do not love you, you are attracted to those who put you down.

You are no longer your own man. You have never

been your own man. Your body has been subjugated and plundered since you were born. Your only home on this earth, this collection of cells that might at least be some brief hymn, some support however disheartened in the sun, this body in which you – you and no one else – will one day die, is not your own. You wage an exhausting campaign, but in your war against the enemy it is yourself you are destroying, little by little, with funereal joy. Your mood swings between disappointment and fear. You are almost happy when you are disappointed, because at least, if only for a moment, you are not afraid. If you carry on like this, your life will have been one long scream between two voids.

And yet, there are moments when you are happy. Maybe you will end up dying prematurely of cirrhosis or an overdose or some other form of abuse, but at least you will have been nothing like your narrow-minded family, like all those people who want to stop you from living your life. It is a June evening, the sky is blue and pink. You walk down the street, your street, with your freedom, paltry and inadequate as it is. It is something hard won, something you snatched from people you thought were invincible. There are buildings, and neon signs flickering, this is a life, and it is here for the taking. You have never bullied anyone, never despised them in the name of some asinine, deadly set of values. You are alive. You look at the pinkish buildings. One day, you won't be here to see them. But today, the sight of these extravagant, fleeting treasures has been granted to you and you alone, and no one can claim to be here in your place.

The street is a river of urban adventures. The air is warm and fraternal. The world is not an outright enemy. Neighbours slap you on the shoulder. Café owners greet you: 'Hey, uncle, will we be seeing you tonight?' Of course, of course! Tonight, you will go and finish this book in every bar in the world, on the gleaming bars, without thinking of love, in the lipsticked face of alcohol. Drinking, loving, living, what's the difference? It is all the same magnificent bullshit. You will smile vaguely, a smile imprinted on your lips by the rim of your glass.

You will go, hard as the times that are in it, with an oblivious and pliant heart, free from all moral concerns, among the bodies masturbated in light who collide and forget each other. The diners laugh. Telephones ring. Behind the laughter, *rien ne va plus*. Love is made and unmade like fortunes on the stock exchange. This is the age of mediocrity. The more mediocre the times, the greater the disappointment. Lonely hearts beat silently, side by side, in suppressed or still unconscious rage. The explosion is imminent.